KILLER'S CHOICE

Killer's Choice

LOUIS BEGLEY

Nan A. Talese | DOUBLEDAY

NEW YORK

Copyright © 2019 by Louis Begley 2007 Revocable Trust

All rights reserved. Published in the United States by Nan A. Talese/ Doubleday, a division of Penguin Random House LLC, New York, and distributed in Canada by Penguin Random House Canada Limited, Toronto.

www.nanatalese.com

DOUBLEDAY is a registered trademark of Penguin Random House LLC. Nan A. Talese and the colophon are trademarks of Penguin Random House LLC.

LIBRARY OF CONGRESS CATALOGING-IN-PUBLICATION DATA
Names: Begley, Louis, author.
Title: Killer's choice : a novel / by Louis Begley.
Description: First edition. | New York : Nan A. Talese, [2019] |
Identifiers: LCCN 2018034306 (print) | LCCN 2018035348 (ebook) |
    ISBN 9780385544948 (hardcover) | ISBN 9780385544955 (ebook)
Subjects: | GSAFD: Suspense fiction.
Classification: LCC PS3552.E373 (ebook) | LCC PS3552.E373 K56 2019
    (print) | DDC 813/.54--dc23
LC record available at https://lccn.loc.gov/2018034306

Book design by Peter A. Andersen
Jacket design by Michael J. Windsor
Jacket images: cage © silavsale/Shutterstock;
man © blackred/E+/Getty Images; sunset © Vicki Jauron,
Babylon and Beyond Photography/Moment/Getty Images

MANUFACTURED IN THE UNITED STATES OF AMERICA

10 9 8 7 6 5 4 3 2 1

First Edition

Once again, for Anka and Adam,

my wonderful first responder readers,

and for Grisha

Hush a by Baby
On the Tree Top
When the Wind blows
The cradle will rock.
If the bough breaks
The cradle will fall,
Down tumbles baby
Cradle and all.

—MOTHER GOOSE'S MELODY

KILLER'S CHOICE

I

There is no end of me, Abner Brown had mocked minutes before he injected himself with the deadly overdose of insulin. I've seen to that! There never will be.

I took those words then to be more of the braggadocio the diabolical Texas billionaire had been spouting ever since I dumped on his desk the files I said I would deliver the next day to the U.S. attorney. Files certain to put Abner behind bars for the rest of his life, or on death row if they helped prove that he had used interstate means to commission murders. Words I was glad to forget. It crossed my mind, not for the first time, that he was insane.

But I am getting ahead of my story. My name is Jack Dana. I am a former Marine Corps Infantry officer and a graduate of its toughest combat schools. The Force Recon platoon I commanded was on patrol in Helmand Province, Afghanistan, near Delaram, when a Taliban sniper got me. His bullet did serious damage to my pelvis. It took a good deal of time and surgeons' skill to make me almost as good as new, although not good enough for active duty with Corps Infantry. When Walter Reed Army Medical Center finally released me, I could have gone back to the fancy academic career on which I had embarked before 9/11 and before I decided to join the marines so as not to leave the fighting to poor saps who hadn't had my sort of privileged upbringing and didn't know any better. But while in the hospital, I began writing about what the wars in Iraq and Afghanistan had been like, and what they had done to my men and me. Completing that book became my only goal. I did finish it, living in New York with my uncle Harry Dana, a prominent lawyer who was like a father to me. Closer to me than my real father. He was also the last living member of my family. My book turned out to be an immediate success; the advance I received, the royalties that followed, the sale of the movie rights, and the bonus to which I became entitled when the movie turned out to be a runaway hit all made me rich. The novels that followed were almost equally successful.

So without my having planned it, writing became my profession.

Once again, I'm getting ahead of the story. Soon after my first book came out, while I was vacationing in Brazil on a fazenda without Internet or cell-phone connection, my uncle Harry was murdered. The murder, disguised as a suicide by hanging, was committed by a hit man called Slobo commissioned by Abner Brown, who had been Harry's principal client. The following day, the same hit man killed Harry's longtime secretary. He pushed her under a subway train. I avenged those murders, as well as the murder, months later, of Kerry Black, my uncle's favorite associate and later young partner, who had helped me get the goods on Brown, the file I gave to the U.S. attorney that led to Abner's ultimate defeat. We had fallen in love passionately, but she dumped me after I killed Slobo instead of only disabling that thug and turning him over to the police. It was murder that Kerry told me I'd committed, and not homicide in legitimate self-defense. Poor Kerry! Abner did not forget the role she played in helping me assemble the dossier laying bare his criminal affair. He had her murdered too, murder disguised this time as her having overdosed on a lethal mixture of drugs.

I was not able to kill Kerry's assassin. Abner had him murdered before I could find him. But once I knew that thug was dead, once I had seen Abner give himself that fatal injection, I stopped thinking about Abner and his crimes. I was tired. Tired of Abner and of the killing I'd done to even the score with him and to stop his hit men, of whom he seemed to have an inexhaustible supply, from killing me. Yes, the wounds I had suffered in the encounter with the last of that lot had healed, but even flesh wounds that require only minimal surgery and heal without major complications take some squeak out of you—my poor lovely mother's favorite expression. Besides, I was absorbed by work on a new book.

In that book, about the murder of my uncle Harry, I told the truth—I declared on the first page that I was telling a true story. For some reviewers what the murderer, Slobo, had done and my duty to avenge my uncle weighed little in comparison with society's interest in bringing Slobo to justice, giving him his day in court. Didn't I know that this is the United States of America, where the rule of law prevails? You bet! The same rule of law that lets billionaires like Abner Brown send rivers of money to PACs and think tanks backing every extreme right-wing cause they can find or dream up and buy and put in their pocket a good half of the U.S. Congress. The rivers of money that have corrupted American politics so thoroughly that a candidate as grotesquely unfit as Donald J. Trump could become president. That kind of rule of law is not good enough for me. I didn't go to war to make America great again—it was plenty great, so far as I was concerned. I wanted America to be decent again. A country that gives suckers an even break, that cares for the weak and needy. If I had still had Slobo or Abner on my mind after my book's appearance, I might have taken out a full-page ad in *The New York Times Book Review* promising solemnly to deal in the future with hit men sent by extremist nuts and their employers exactly as I had dealt with Slobo and his employer.

But I wasn't thinking about any of that. I was obsessed by the damage the Trump administration was doing to the country at home and abroad. Every thought I could spare was for a girl with whom I was head over heels in love: an impossibly lovely, elegant, and clever lady litigator, Heidi Krohn. Heidi had been Kerry's best friend. She became my partner in the quest to avenge Kerry and destroy Abner. But, from the first, she set the rules. She was not attracted physically to men, she warned me when we first met. It hadn't always been so, she said, and it might not be so forever. We shook hands on that, and, in time, I came to have grounds to think that for once

I was playing my cards right: patience and forbearance were paying off. Just a few weeks after Abner died, Heidi spent the Christmas vacation with me at the house in Sag Harbor I inherited from my uncle Harry. I gave her the master bedroom, thinking that I would occupy a guest room across the hall, but she invited me to share her bed. Only to "cuddle," she specified. We have cuddled ever since, of late dispensing with the tops of our pajamas, and, although she didn't give up her pad on Lexington and Eighty-Seventh, many weekday nights she could be found at my Fifth Avenue apartment, another property I inherited from Uncle Harry. If we decided to go to the country, she'd stay at my house in Sag Harbor, paying only brief visits to her parents, whose house is in East Hampton on Further Lane. And she brought over to Fifth Avenue much of her wondrous wardrobe and the true love of her life, a coal-black one-and-a-half-year-old French bulldog named Satan. It's much better for him to be with you, across the street from Central Park, than to sit alone all day at my apartment waiting for the walker to take him out. These were the surest signs, I believe, that we were on the right track.

The call came shortly after eleven, on a Wednesday night. She was once again in Hong Kong, leading the defense in an arbitration brought against a new client, a huge Japanese construction company. I had tried to work on my new book, had dinner at home, and when the phone rang had been about to go to bed. Picking up the receiver, I expected to hear her voice—I could think of no one else who'd call at that hour—but instead I heard screams. Screams more awful than any I had ever heard. Worse than the screaming of marines in Iraq or Afghanistan with limbs torn off by an IED or stomach wounds so bad the intestines were exposed, worse than the howling of a Taliban prisoner in Delaram some CIA contractors were working over, they rose in unbearable crescendo. Transfixed with horror, I didn't hang up. After a time, which then seemed interminable but, in reality, was no more than five minutes, a man's deep voice addressed me. Loud enough to be heard over the screaming.

Nice, the man said, your friends scream good. Boss said let him listen and enjoy.

He fell silent. I couldn't stop listening or bring myself to hang up.

He spoke again.

So long now. We keep working.

Again, he fell silent, but the screams continued, louder and, if possible, even more desperate. Then the line went dead.

I pressed the Off button on the receiver and feverishly—my hands were trembling—scrolled down to the list of incoming calls. The most recent was from Simon Lathrop, followed by a 917 telephone number.

Simon Lathrop, my uncle Harry's law partner, law school classmate, and best friend! My cell phone was on the desk. I navigated to Contacts, typed in Simon's name, and found the address and telephone number of his weekend house in Bedford. The telephone numbers were identical. No, this could not be some macabre joke. I had to get through to the local police—without wasting a moment. I called 911 and was transferred to the Bedford Police Department. I told the female dispatcher that I believed a gruesome crime was being committed at Mr. Simon Lathrop's house. She knew who he was and where he lived and took down my name, address, and telephone number.

I'm sending a cruiser over there right away, she said, and I'll be in touch with the chief.

Judging by what I heard on the phone, I told her, you probably want more than one officer at that house.

You may be right, she replied. We'll see what we can do.

Good luck, I said. I'm taking my car and should be at the Lathrops' within the hour.

I talked my way past a cordon of cops and state troopers and got to the front porch of the house. There, a corpulent civilian in his fifties introduced himself as Assistant D.A. Steve Bruni of the Investigations Division and said, You're Captain Dana. I've read your book *Returning,* and I've seen the movie. First-rate. I'm a fan. Look, I know about your service with the marines and I know you've seen a lot of killing. Guess you've done some yourself, including those two hit men in Sag Harbor. Yes, I looked you up as soon as I heard the perpetrators called you and you were coming over. But what we've got here is not like any crime scene I've seen in my career, and I've seen plenty. Before this job, when I was a special agent, I worked on organized crime. It's worse than the photos of the Manson family and Sharon Tate. A real cult massacre. I doubt you've seen anything like it either and I'm not sure you want to look at it.

I think I have to, I answered. Simon Lathrop was a friend.

All right, just remember I warned you. They did a job on the house too.

The house is a big white Victorian structure. I followed Bruni inside and, as soon as we entered, I saw what Bruni meant. Someone had gone through the ground-floor rooms with a baseball bat or an ax and a knife, breaking furniture, taking paintings off the walls and kicking them in, and slashing the cushions of sofas and armchairs.

Bruni spoke again: The bodies are upstairs, in the master bedroom. We've got people everywhere taking photographs and looking for fingerprints and all the other usual stuff.

Indeed, the house was swarming with state troopers and civilians.

I pointed with my chin at the civilians and raised my eyebrows.

FBI, Bruni told me. When I told the D.A. what went on here, he called the Manhattan assistant Bureau head at home and asked the FBI to step in on a provisional basis. He thinks this has the hallmarks of an organized-crime job. You'll see. Jack Curley doesn't let grass grow under his feet, and the Lathrops are important people.

He paused at the door of the bedroom and said, Now fasten your seat belt. The bodies are as we found them.

Bruni was right: I've seen my share of dead bodies, including bodies torn apart by explosions or cut into pieces by heavy machine-gun fire. But none of them matched what had been done to Simon and Jennie Lathrop. They were both naked. Simon had been crucified, nailed to a closet door, four- or five-inch spikes through his hands and feet. His penis and testicles had been sliced off. Most of his skin had been flayed, long strips left hanging.

This took time, Bruni observed. They slit his throat. That probably came at the end as they left. Some coup de grâce!

I nodded. I don't think I was capable of speech.

Jennie was on the bed. Her breasts had been cut off. Looking at her, I realized that the closet door to which Simon was nailed faced the bed, so that he would have seen every detail of what was done to her and, indeed, I now noticed that her breast lay on the floor, at Simon's feet. She'd been raped—no other word came into my mind—with a thick stick that had been left lying on the bed, and perhaps with other objects too. Her thighs were covered with blood. The bedding was soaked with blood. They hadn't flayed her. Instead, they had used a cruder form of torture. Her body was covered with burns. Some seemed like cigarette burns; others were round but probably too big to have been made with a cigarette. Her fingernails had been pulled out. The pliers too had been left on the bed.

Steady, Captain Dana, Bruni said, I told you this was bad. And it must have taken a long time. They made it take a long time.

Yes, I answered. Yes, there must have been at least two of them.

Bruni nodded. Yes, perhaps more.

Any fingerprints, anything that might identify them?

So far, zero. But we'll give the house another going-over tomorrow morning. The bodies will stay here until we've finished. And no tire tracks or anything like them outside. As you saw, we parked way down the driveway, to leave the turn-around outside the house undisturbed. They didn't break in. Either Mr. Lathrop let them in, or the door was open, or they had a pretty good set of passkeys. By the way, can you identify the bodies for us?

Of course, I said.

That's helpful. The D.A. would like to speak to you tomorrow afternoon. The office is in White Plains. Do you think you can be there at two?

Of course, I said again. I'll be there.

The identification formalities finished, Bruni gave me his card with the office address and telephone numbers on it. We shook hands, and, as I turned to leave, he said, Look, Captain Dana, I know you can take care of yourself, but this is very bad stuff. Be on your guard!

Feng, my combination houseman, gourmet cook, and, ever since he shot, in the nick of time, the last of the killers Abner had sent to finish me off, my savior and self-appointed bodyguard, greeted me at the door of my apartment. It was a few minutes past five in the morning. I had driven back to the city from Bedford very slowly, trying both to erase from my field of vision the images of Simon and Jennie and to begin to make sense of what had happened. This savage attack on a dignified, honorable old couple: Who would have chosen them as the target? Who would have carried it out? What was the meaning of the telephone call to me? Yes, Simon was my friend, but our perfectly cordial contacts were infrequent. He was an important senior partner at Jones & Whetstone, a leading New York City law firm, a fixture on the boards of the Metropolitan Museum and the Metropolitan Opera and probably other great cultural institutions in the city. He and Jennie were sociable, mentioned regularly in the press as attending this or that charity dinner or ball. If the idea was to spread terror among their acquaintances, I was willing to bet there were at least twenty people on terms of more intimate friendship with them.

I didn't know, sir, Feng said, that you intended to go out after dinner and to stay out so very late. If I may say so, I was concerned about you.

His tone was, as always, perfect. He wasn't complaining or scolding. Merely stating the facts.

I'm very sorry, Feng, I replied. I should have left you a note. The fact is that I left unexpectedly and in a great hurry. I'll explain it all at breakfast.

It was clear that Feng should be informed. My respect for the loyalty and cool nerve of this former member of the Hong Kong Police Force Special Duty Unit—a SWAT team probably better known as Flying Tigers—who'd made himself loathed by the mainland authorities by pushing forward with an investigation they wanted him to drop, had continued to grow. I would want to know his take on what had happened, and, why not admit it, I didn't mind knowing that he'd have my back.

Thank you, sir. Breakfast can be ready in ten minutes.

Give me half an hour, I replied. I'd like to get out of these clothes and take a hot bath. I'll have breakfast in the kitchen.

Feng's breakfast menus ranged from orange juice, whole-wheat toast and bitter-orange marmalade, and coffee, through congee with crullers, steamed stuffed buns, and boiled eggs, all the way to what I considered hearty English fare. Usually, I asked him to stick to the whole-wheat-toast solution. That morning I expressed no preference and when I came into the kitchen was greeted by grapefruit juice, coddled eggs and bacon, and croissants (Feng apologized for their having been frozen), and a very large pot of coffee, the aroma of which alone would have sufficed to clear my head. I prevailed on him to make himself some tea—I knew that was the beverage he preferred—and to sit down with me at the table.

It's an ugly story, Feng, I said, and proceeded to tell him everything, from the telephone call to the end of my conversation with Bruni.

After a moment of silence, Feng spoke.

I believe Mr. Bruni is right. We will have to be very careful. These are dangerous people. I believe they will try to harm you.

But why, Feng? I asked. What is the reason you think they are after me?

It's that telephone call, sir. It was made for a purpose. To tell you that something like it could happen to you. If I may make a request, sir, please let me drive you out to White Plains and bring you back home.

I made an effort to clear the cobwebs from my brain.

Thank you, Feng, I said, I would like that. And now I'm going to try to get some sleep—but not past eleven.

II

Bruni met me at the reception desk and guided me past security.

Jack Curley, the D.A., is waiting, he said. With a bunch of people: New York office of the FBI, the Bedford police chief, and a couple of guys from the New York State Bureau of Criminal Investigation. They're plainclothes state cops who work on violent crimes. Also, the D.A.'s chief of staff. By the way, as you may have noticed, there is nothing in the press, printed or online, and nothing on TV. The D.A. has embargoed everything about the massacre until after he has interviewed you. So far, it's worked.

I had in fact looked at the online *New York Times* Breaking News and seen nothing.

Not quite sure whether I was supposed to be grateful, I asked whether there were any developments.

A big fat zero. No fresh fingerprints other than the Lathrops' and the housekeeper's. Luckily for her, she doesn't live in. If she'd been there, they'd have surely killed her too. Nothing in the toilets, no footprints. Really nothing. Here, it's this door. He knocked, and we entered.

A gray-haired man in his late fifties or early sixties sat at what by virtue of his presence seemed to be the head of a large oval conference table littered with Starbucks cups and paper plates holding remains of sandwiches. Clearly, the D.A. Bruni introduced me. The D.A. asked the other participants to identify themselves and motioned for me to sit across from him. Bruni took his place on his right, next to the FBI man. The BCI representatives and the Bedford chief were on his left.

We'll get right down to business, Mr. Dana, said the D.A. If you don't object, this interview will be recorded.

That's fine.

Thank you! By the way, Mr. Edwards—that was the name of the FBI representative—is here because this crime has some of the hallmarks of organized-crime involvement. That's just to explain the Bureau's potential involvement in a murder case. I should also tell you that I've explained to the group who you are—some of us have read your books and are fans—and reminded them that there were two attempts on your life. Both in your house in Sag Harbor. Both times you managed to kill the assailant. Based on interviews you gave at the time and your most recent novel, which you state is a true account, I take it you believe that both attempts were linked to the murder of your uncle Harry Dana in the same house in Sag Harbor, some months before the first attempt on your life. Is that correct?

Yes, it is.

And to your uncle's having collected evidence showing that businesses owned or controlled by his former client Abner Brown, and Abner Brown himself, were engaged in a variety of criminal activities, and to your uncle's presumed intention to deliver this evidence to law-enforcement authorities. Is that also correct?

Yes.

In fact, your uncle having been murdered, it fell to you to deliver this evidence to the U.S. attorney for the Southern District, as well as additional evidence that came into your hands after your uncle's death. Correct?

In substance, yes, I replied, but this was a complicated series of events.

The D.A. was clearly reading questions written out on the sheet before him, at which he kept glancing, and wasn't about to go off script.

Quite right. We may have to get into those complications at some point, though perhaps not this afternoon. In the meantime, could you confirm the report we've had from Bedford police chief Mahoney. In relevant part it indicates that the dispatcher on duty received a call from you yesterday, at 2322 hours, in the course of which you stated that a violent crime was being committed at the domicile of Mr. and Mrs. Simon Lathrop on Penwood Road in Bedford Corners. Correct?

Yes.

Would you tell us how you acquired that knowledge? Mr.

Bruni gave us his recollection of what you told him at the scene of the crime, but we would all like to hear it for the record from your own mouth.

Certainly, I answered. It was a telephone call I received at home. After the caller hung up, I immediately used the caller-ID function of the telephone and saw that it was made on Simon Lathrop's line, from his Westchester residence. Then I dialed 911. The duration of the call I received? Not more than five or six minutes.

I went on to describe the screaming and the voice that addressed me.

Have you any idea who the "boss" referred to by the voice might be?

I don't, I answered. I have absolutely no idea.

Will you tell us about your relationship with Mr. and Mrs. Lathrop?

He was my uncle Harry Dana's best friend at his law firm, Jones & Whetstone, and his classmate at Harvard Law School. I believe they were both taken into the firm as partners the same year. I met Mr. Lathrop and also Mrs. Lathrop at a book party my uncle gave for my first novel. I saw Mr. Lathrop at lunch several times after my uncle's murder. He was helpful in some ways with regard to the files detailing Abner Brown's crimes that I turned over to Mr. Flanagan, the U.S. attorney for the Southern District. I've also had dinner with the Lathrops at their apartment in the city. Perhaps three times.

I decided I'd stop there. I had never told Ed Flanagan that I had given Abner copies of the files that the next day I delivered to him, and that I was present while Abner read them and discovered the extent of his ruin, and while he injected himself with the fatal dose of insulin, or that it was Simon who told me that Abner would be in the city that particular day. I hadn't wanted to volunteer that information. But I had no doubt that if any of Flanagan's questions had called for it, I wouldn't have held it back. The fact was that he hadn't asked, and now I felt queasy about telling Curley more than I had told Flanagan. It was possible that those two would talk, and I didn't want to put Flanagan in the awkward position of hearing facts from Curley that he might consider material to his investigation but had failed to elicit.

That's pretty straightforward, the D.A. said. Let's move on. You saw the crime scene yesterday. Can you think of anyone—let's assume that it's someone sick and depraved—who might have a sufficient motive to commit or organize this slaughter?

This is a question I've been asking myself, I answered. The fact is that I can't. Mr. Lathrop was a fine old-fashioned gentleman, kind and charming. That's based on the limited social contact we'd had. According to what my uncle told me, he was also an exceedingly able and highly respected lawyer. Really, a lovely man. Not someone who would have been involved with criminals of this sort.

And then the thought came into my head, and I raised my hand as though in a class asking permission to speak.

There's one thing, though, I should perhaps mention, Mr. Curley, I said. It has just occurred to me that it may be relevant. When I began to look into the circumstances of my uncle Harry Dana's death, I realized that a very considerable effort had been made on behalf of the person who was then the chairman of his law firm, one William Hobson, to search my uncle's personal papers at his New York apartment and at his Sag Harbor house. Also, his personal papers at the law firm had simply disappeared. Then I discovered that in order to push my uncle out of the firm, to force him to retire, Hobson had spread among the partners the rumor that my uncle had become demented or senile. That was absolutely untrue. I made Mr. Lathrop aware of all this. He was outraged. His own inquiry confirmed what I had said and led him to believe that Hobson and his brother-in-law, another partner in the firm who specialized in trusts and estates, one Fred Minot, had behaved unethically, unprofessionally—I don't remember how else he qualified their behavior. As a result, he and a group of other seniors did whatever was necessary to fire Hobson from the firm. Hobson, by the way, had been my uncle's second-in-command on Abner Brown's legal matters. It was Mr. Lathrop's belief that Hobson had moved against my uncle at Brown's behest. Anyway, Hobson and Minot left and became partners in a Houston law firm, taking with them Abner Brown's very considerable legal business. I'm mentioning all this because Hobson and Minot are the only two people I know of who surely had it in for Mr. Lathrop. But to go from there to what happened on Penwood Road seems far-fetched and grotesque.

That's probably true, said the D.A., but you were right to bring these circumstances to our attention.

I've just Googled Hobson, said Edwards. His current business position is chairman of the board of Abner Brown Holdings. That would seem to be the top company in the Brown business structure. We'll want to look into the share ownership and related matters.

The D.A. nodded. A good idea. Going back to you, Mr. Dana, have you thought why whoever placed the call—presumably one of the murderers—would have telephoned you and have you listen to the screams. You said that he told you that the boss wanted you to listen. Have you any idea of who the boss might be?

Let me start with your second question, I replied. As I've said before, I don't, I have absolutely no idea about who the boss might be. As to your first question, it's one I've been asking myself ever since, and the only answer I've been able to come up with is that someone wants to frighten me, to give me a warning. But a warning about what? Who would want to frighten me? I don't know. Abner Brown had his hit men or other underlings send me messages such as "You're next" or "You're roadkill"—sick stuff spawned by his weird sense of humor. But he is dead. Dead men don't send messages or stage macabre Punch-and-Judy shows.

No, they don't, Curley agreed, directing a level look at me. But people who want to avenge them might, if there are such people and they're sufficiently crazy. People who see you as the architect of Abner Brown's downfall, perhaps his death. I've looked at the clippings about his death from the insulin overdose. People with type one diabetes, who have been injecting the stuff most of their lives, aren't likely to inject an overdose by mistake. One might consider whether he didn't do it on purpose, in order to take his own life.

This wasn't a question, and I remained silent.

Meanwhile, the D.A. was trying to be helpful. I believe you're right to think that whoever organized these murders and the telephone call to you wants to frighten you. We can't predict the next move here. But the method chosen is so extreme, and the murders are so gruesome, that I believe you may be personally in danger. Do you agree?

I certainly agree that we can't predict the next move or whether there is going to be any next move, I answered. As for my being personally in danger, I understand your concern and I intend to be careful. The question is, Careful about what? And how?

The D.A. nodded and said, Here is what I think: You are implicitly under threat, and my recommendation is that you be given police protection. I think that Captain Morrison can arrange it through his contacts at the New York Police Department.

Glad to do it, replied the senior Bureau of Criminal Investigation guy.

I'm very grateful, I replied, but I really think this is unnecessary and premature. I'm pretty good at taking care of myself, and I have working for me as housekeeper a Hong Kong Chinese man, Feng Houzhi, who is a former member of the Hong Kong Police Force's equivalent of a SWAT team. He was recommended to me by a retired FBI special agent, Martin Sweeney, with whom I've worked, and by my closest friend, who works for the CIA and is familiar with Feng's case. As I understand it, Feng has a solid record with the FBI that you can surely access. If not, I can get Martin Sweeney to help. Feng is the best bodyguard I could have, and if Captain Morrison or another one of you gentlemen could help him to obtain on an expedited basis a concealed carry license for a handgun, that would be an enormous help. Feng is a permanent resident of the U.S. but not yet a citizen.

I know Martin well, interjected Edwards, and will reach out to him.

We'll go off the record, said the D.A., but before we do there is one more thing. If anything happens in relation to you that has a bearing on this case, please report it promptly to Mr. Bruni and Mr. Edwards. This is of the greatest importance. May we count on your cooperation?

It seemed impossible to say anything other than yes, so that is what I said.

Thank you, replied the D.A. as he turned off the recording device, and continued, We will certainly help Mr. Feng. Mr. Bruni will orchestrate this with the help of the Bureau, for which we're all grateful. At the same time, I would urge you to reconsider the offer of organizing police protection for you. Whatever we're dealing with here is very ugly.

I will think about it, I replied, and I want to stress that I'm very grateful. May I ask how you and the other gentlemen here intend to proceed given what I understand to be the absence of any clues at the murder scene?

Police work, police work, and more police work, replied the Bedford chief. And hope for a lucky break. Speaking of luck, we've been lucky here in this county. We haven't had a murder anything like this, not in my memory. I guess we all recall the Petit case over in Connecticut almost ten years ago. That was almost as brutal as what happened on Penwood Road, but the perpetrators were drifters. What we have here is a targeted, organized attack.

Edwards and the senior Bureau of Criminal Investigation guy nodded in agreement.

The silence was broken by the D.A. We want you alive, he said with a cheerless sort of smile. So please be careful!

Then he thanked me for my cooperation and wished me luck.

By the way, he added, I've kept the media out of this so as not to get you involved in the inevitable circus, but we'll lift the embargo now, except for the telephone call you received. We will treat that as highly confidential.

I called Feng on his cell phone as soon as I was out of the building, and within what seemed like seconds he pulled up. I got into the Volvo's passenger seat and gratefully accepted the thermos of coffee he handed me.

Is there anything new, sir? Feng asked.

Nothing. No fingerprints, no foot marks, absolutely nothing to go on. The FBI is on the case, in addition to the local and the state police. I suppose they hope someone will turn up who has seen the men who might be the killers in the area, perhaps at a gas station, or in some diner. Police work and more police work, they said. I somehow doubt that they'll get anywhere.

I do too, sir.

As Feng coped expertly with the chaotic afternoon traffic, the realization came upon me that I was afraid. The fear was different from any I had ever experienced in Iraq or Afghanistan, in combat or on patrol. That was fear of explosions blowing your vehicle sky-high and you with it, of mortar shells and sniper fire. It receded with the first rush of adrenaline when you went on the attack. This was something radically different: fear as sick as what had been done to the Lathrops, filthy, clammy, and pervasive. It's true, what I said to the D.A.: Dead men don't send messages. But Abner had warned me. There would be no end of him. That was, of course, ridiculous, but both the D.A. and Feng seemed to see all the hallmarks of a vendetta in what had happened. Why had I missed them? To the fear was now added a growing sense of my obtuseness. What was it that Eric King, the former sharpshooter noncom in my Force Recon platoon, turned Abner Brown's hit man, said before he drew his Ka-Bar and went for my neck? You're not as quick on the uptake as you used to be, Captain Dana, that's what he said, and he was goddam right. Abner's threat, whatever it meant, could be real.

III

Strongly encouraged by Feng, I lay down when we got home and slept for more than two hours. A heavy dreamless sleep, from which I awoke rested and calm. D.A. Curley thought I might be the next target. Feng thought the same. Great minds think alike. What was the taunt George W. hurled at Iraqi insurgents just about the time I was getting ready to deploy to Al Anbar Province? Bring 'em on! They sure did, and we sure came to regret it. I recalled Dubya's words as I thought of the goons who'd butchered Simon and Jennie Lathrop and the monster who had sent them. Was I saying to him, Bring 'em on? Was I about to become as great a fool as our forty-third president? The old me would have said, So be it! Make yourself a decoy. Let them come after you. How else would Captain Morrison or Chief Mahoney or the FBI man whose name I'd forgotten find these goons who'd left no traces other than the havoc and carnage they had wrought? That Jack Dana maneuver had worked just fine when I wanted to kill the son of a bitch who had murdered Harry and worked almost as well on the son of a bitch Abner sent to murder me. But back then I was on missions—first to avenge my uncle and later a woman I had loved—I couldn't go AWOL from them, not if I wanted to be able to bear the sight of my face in the mirror. But the slaughter of the Lathrops? That was different. I had been fond of Simon and Jennie, but why should I not leave this crime to the local and state cops, especially since the FBI, presumably as good a police force as any notwithstanding the diatribes of our deranged president, was also involved? Why should I pretend I'm some sort of super sheriff? Basta! I should stick to my writing and try to stay alive.

Soon after Abner died, convinced that my killing days were over, I stashed away my Colt .45 and ammo in the safe, along with the Ka-Bar and the switchblade I got off a crazy mullah I killed in Helmand before he was able to pull the pin out of the grenade with which he'd intended to blow himself up along with my battalion CO, me, and whoever else was in our headquarters tent. I slit his throat with the Ka-Bar. His own razor-sharp knife was a souvenir I cherished and had had occasion to use. I got my tricked-out .45, the extra ammo, and the Ka-Bar and put them in the middle drawer of my library desk. The switchblade would henceforth be my constant companion. It was a friend I could trust. I had absolutely nothing against staying alive.

Curley had sure lifted the press embargo. The Penwood Road Massacre, as the murder of the Lathrops quickly came to be known, was a lead item in *The New York Times* and *The Wall Street Journal* online Breaking News and, I've no doubt, in the tabloids I didn't read. Feng was watching the coverage on ABC when I came into the kitchen, and he told me that the other chains, Fox, and CNN were carrying the story as well. There were no images of the corpses. I thought they must have been removed before the journalists and photographers were admitted—and perhaps there were rules that prevented printing or screening anything so gruesome—but there was ample photo coverage of the havoc in the house, and verbal descriptions of what had been done to the Lathrops so vivid that little was left to the imagination. References to Helter Skelter, the Charles Manson cult-family murder of Sharon Tate, seemed obligatory, as well as speculation about the Lathrops' having perhaps been the victims of a diabolical sect. A couple of the more literary journalists mentioned the Clutter family murders memorialized in Truman Capote's *In Cold Blood* and the movie based on his book, and suggested that the opulence of the Lathrop house and Simon Lathrop's presumed wealth as a senior partner of a top-earning New York City law firm could have prompted a robbery that, as in the case of the Clutters, turned into unspeakable carnage when the robbers' expectations about the cash they'd find were disappointed. The statements of the Bedford chief of police, D.A. Curley's spokesman, and the spokesman for the Manhattan office of the FBI were all the same pablum: the investigation was preliminary; there were no clues or motives that could be discussed at this stage; full resources would be devoted to solving this shocking crime and bringing the malefactors to justice. That more than one assailant was involved was taken for granted. I was struck by the absence of any mention of—or even a veiled allusion to—me and the telephone call I had received. Curley had kept his word.

At seven-thirty, Feng served the usual perfect gin martini in the library, accompanied this time by stuffed eggs, and announced that he had taken it on himself to settle the dinner menu: wonton soup, the chicken with red peppers that he knew I liked, and early strawberries that were quite sweet.

A light meal, he observed. You'll be able, sir, to get a good night's sleep. If I may say so, it's what you need.

I apologized for my absentmindedness and explained that my plan, which I had forgotten to mention, had been to have dinner at the usual Italian restaurant on Third Avenue so he wouldn't have to cook after an afternoon wasted in White Plains.

I would strongly advise you not to go out, sir, Feng answered. I truly believe you are in great danger and shouldn't go out alone, not until you have approved appropriate security precautions. I've worked on many cases involving Hong Kong triads. They're our criminal gangs, still very powerful even if you don't hear much about them since the PRC took over the colony. I've found that when they want to terrorize a target, there will be a first attack and then very soon a second attack. Sometimes a third. I hope you will forgive me: half an hour ago, I took Satan out for his walk without asking your permission. I know that you like to have the evening stroll with him, but for the moment it is more prudent for him to walk with me.

Satan was settled in his favorite corner of the sofa, catty-corner from me, his huge eyes fixed on me, following the conversation attentively and making dismissive guttural French-bulldog noises. Satan was a lucky little fellow. Heidi adored him. It goes without saying that I'd gotten to love him. But so had Feng and every doorman, front- and rear-elevator man, and handyman in the building. His special friend Brian, the afternoon doorman, told me he was the building's mascot.

I understand, I said. Let me think about it for a while. We'll talk after dinner.

Dinner was up to Feng's highest standards. I asked for seconds of the wonton soup and devoured the chicken. I too was a lucky fellow. Heidi was sharing my bed; my prep-school and Yale classmate, Scott Prentice, now high up in the CIA, the sort of brother I would have wished to have, was still my best friend, one as ready to take a bullet for me as I was ready to take one for him; I was the godfather of his firstborn son; and I had working for me the admirable Feng. He'd saved my life once, and, I was sure, would save my life again if the need arose.

When he brought my usual after-dinner espresso into the library, I suggested that he make himself a cup of green tea and join me there.

Please sit down, I said when he returned. We'll have our

talk about danger and how to respond, I added. For the first time today, my head is clear. Satan will need to go out, but he can wait until we've finished.

For once, Feng didn't resist my invitation to sit down comfortably in the club armchair across the coffee table from me.

Good, I said. Let's talk. Tell me how you think we should deal with this situation.

With all due respect, sir, I am reminded of what I believe was the pattern when Mr. Abner Brown was alive. Telephone or letter threats followed by an attack.

You're right about the threats at that time, but Brown is dead, I protested. Dead. Incinerated. His ashes scattered. All as duly reported by the *Houston Chronicle.*

Yes, sir, that is true, but there may be people who want to avenge him. It's possible that they murdered Mr. and Mrs. Lathrop because he was your friend and helped you—I understand that was the case—and the additional reason may be to show you what you can expect for yourself. If they are Abner Brown's friends, they may like using some of his methods. I have seen the top triads in Hong Kong operate that way. Intimidation followed by extortion or an attack.

I see, I replied. Connecting this new horror to Abner Brown or anyone close to him seems both plausible and very far-fetched. And what do you think I should do?

If I may, sir, I would like to make some suggestions.

Please do, I replied.

They're very simple, sir. First, I think you should avoid going out alone. I don't mean such things as going to the gym.

But please allow me to accompany you when you go running in Central Park. I am also concerned about your walking Satan in the park and also on Fifth Avenue, especially on the park side. You pay close attention to Satan and I fear you can't be as alert to danger signals as you should be. They may use Satan to distract you. For instance, someone kicks him. Another person attacks you from the back. Second, please let me accompany you and Miss Heidi when you go to Sag Harbor for weekends. We know that the house isn't secure but, if I am there, you and I should be able to avoid being surprised and should be able to repel an attack. Third, please explain the situation to Miss Heidi and ask her to explain it to her father. She needs protection by his security service. The father and the rest of the family need protection as well. If I may say so, I hope you will bring Mr. Scott Prentice up-to-date and that you will consider asking Mr. Martin Sweeney to provide additional security.

Her father's and grandfather's clothes-manufacturing and real estate businesses had made Heidi's father a billionaire, and the family firm, Krohn Enterprises, had a security force of their own consisting of former special agents, Mossad operatives, and similar worthies. He had assigned a detail to hover over her when Abner's offensive against me gathered steam.

A wave of discouragement swept over me as I listened to him. Feng's and D.A. Curley's views of the Penwood Road Massacre coincided disturbingly. Yes, the telephone call could mean only one thing, that those murders were somehow related to me, intended to scare me or as a warning, it didn't much matter which, and Penwood Road was only the first chapter in a probable succession of murders that some psycho intended to unleash. So much for the tranquil months I had hoped to devote to my new novel, which was, in any case, going badly. For the first time in my short but surprisingly satisfactory writing career, I was stuck. Was it a failure of imagination, and, if that was the cause, was it permanent or could I hope for a rebound? I wasn't optimistic about being able to get the novel going again and had begun to think of turning to a book on the Sicilian wars, best known as the Sicilian Disaster, that Athens plunged into beginning in 415 B.C. and kept fighting until 404, at which point the Athenian empire ceased to exist. It would be a homecoming of sorts, a return to the project I abandoned after 9/11 in order to join the fight. Country and honor: the examples of my father and grandfather had spurred me on, those warriors without an ounce of bellicosity in their bodies, who had fought heroically in World War II and in Vietnam. All that was now beside the point. If I was to stay alive and keep Heidi and Satan out of harm—yes, Satan too, because I remembered how the hit man who tortured and killed my uncle Harry had first tortured his cat, and wrung its neck—I would have to face these murderous thugs and whoever sent them and go back to killing. Perhaps I would avenge the Lathrops even if that was not my mission. Either way, I'd be once again up to my elbows in blood.

These thoughts were interrupted by the telephone. Feng asked if I wanted him to answer and, always discreet, offered to withdraw when I shook my head. I asked him to stay and picked up the receiver. It was Scott Prentice, who had seen coverage of the murders on TV.

You're right, I told him, it's a perfect nightmare and closer to home than you probably imagine. Have you time to hear that part of the story?

He said he did. His wife, Susie, was pregnant with their second child and, feeling tired—my godson Jack was a handful—had gone to bed directly after dinner. He could give me all the time I needed.

The succinct version was clearly enough to rock him. He gave a long whistle and asked for the name of the FBI representative present at the meeting.

Edwards, I think. Or something like it.

The FBI should be involved, Scott continued. I'm glad they were at the meeting. We'll check this Edwards guy out. Our liaison with the Bureau may know him, or if Edwards isn't the right name he'll get the name of the guy who was at the meeting. If necessary, we'll connect you to someone else at the Bureau. This is really bad.

Join the club, I replied. Everyone seems to think so, the Westchester D.A. and Feng included.

If I were you, I'd listen carefully to Feng's advice. He's had a lot of experience with criminal gangs. Let's talk again tomorrow after I've checked around, and for God's sake don't take foolish risks. Not unless you want to be killed.

All right, Shao-Feng, I said after Scott and I had hung up, one point in your program has been taken care of. Scott is on board. Let's go over the others, but first I would like to have some Oban neat.

Shao means "old" in Mandarin. If you attach it as a prefix to someone's name, you signify both respect and affection. Feng had earned both.

Fourteen or eighteen year, sir? he asked.

Who knows how long I'll be around to drink it? I answered. Let's go for the eighteen, and please have some yourself.

Thank you, sir, but with your permission I'll have a drop of Maotai instead.

He returned from the pantry with the drinks and, having been urged again, and finally given a direct order, sat down ramrod straight in a side chair.

All right, I said, I certainly agree that Miss Heidi needs protection and I think you're right about her family as well. Whoever these bastards are, they will clearly stop at nothing. We'll talk to Miss Heidi when she returns. I don't think it's the sort of thing I can discuss with her on the telephone.

Yes, sir. But would you mind if I asked two of my friends in Hong Kong, who were in the Flying Tigers with me, to keep an eye on her? There won't be any charge. Foreigners often think that Hong Kong is a very safe place, and that is true unless bad people have reason to harm you. She wouldn't need to know about it. They will be very discreet.

I would like that very much, but I'd also like to compensate your friends for their time and for taking risks.

That is really unnecessary, sir. They wouldn't accept money for something I ask them to do. They will be happy to help.

All I can say then is thank you! Please assure them of my gratitude. Moving on to the rest of your menu, yes, I think it's a good idea for you to come with Miss Heidi and me when we go to Sag Harbor. Yes, I think you should walk Satan unless something interferes, in which case I'll take him. Martin Sweeney. I'm not sure just what he would do for us. When he last worked for me, it was in order to find out whether I was being tailed. That seems unnecessary now. If you are right that these thugs are after me, I think we can assume that there is a tail or some other system to keep track of my comings and goings. Perhaps we will want to ask Martin to do some real detective work, but I must think through what it is we need that the police and the FBI aren't already doing. All right so far?

Yes, thank you, sir.

Now we're getting to a couple of places where I think you'll disagree. First, coming with me to Sag Harbor when I go there alone. Second, when I go running. You've gotten to know me pretty well, so it won't surprise you that I say I don't want to act scared. I'm not scared, and if it's only my life that's in danger I think I can take care of myself. There is another side to it. If these people want to have a go at me, let them. I may be able to teach them a lesson. On the other hand, if you are always with me—by the way, the D.A. or the state police fellow will pull some strings to get you a concealed carry license—we may make it too difficult for them to play around. They may think they have to go for something we can't repel. Perhaps instead of sending a hit man I can most probably handle, they may go for sending a sniper with a high-powered rifle. Yes, I'll be taking a risk, but it's a risk worth taking. One final thing: I don't think the police or the FBI will catch these thugs. Letting them attack me may be the only way to make contact and catch them or in some other way to make sure they never kill again.

Forgive me, sir. These people are too dangerous. I think more dangerous than the people who worked for Mr. Abner Brown.

Look, Feng, let me try it. We can always change our minds or our tactics.

I think he was going to argue with me—something that went against his impeccable manners—or perhaps even offer a retort, such as Sure, if you're still alive, when the telephone rang. Close to eleven. It could be Heidi, or it could be them. I picked up the receiver. The caller-ID window showed a whole lot of numbers. That would be Hong Kong. I pressed the Talk button and heard Heidi's voice.

I know, she said. I've read the story in the *Times*. *The Guardian* carried it as well. You must feel awful.

I do, I told her. They were such good people and they suffered so horribly.

I decided that I wouldn't tell her over the telephone about the call to me or my having been to Penwood Road or the sinister consensus that had developed as to the implications of these murders for me. Instead, I filled her in on Satan's most recent exploits and digestion, which happened to be excellent, and asked about her arbitration. I yearned for her to come back—tomorrow or the day after, if possible—but knew I shouldn't pressure her.

With a note of triumph in her voice, one I know she tried

to conceal, she replied that the case was going well for her side, so well that the arbitrators decided to extend the hearings by ten days and hear proof of South Korean law that the other side had argued strenuously was unnecessary.

Bravo! I answered, summoning all the enthusiasm I could manage, and asked whether she'd be free to return as soon as the hearings ended.

Not quite, was her answer. She'd have to stop in Tokyo on the way home, to report on the hearings to the clients' top management.

You wouldn't think that was necessary, she continued, there were six Japanese "staffs," as they like to call themselves, representing the legal department and, again as they say, the "relevant" business departments, each of them as stiff as a real staff, attending every session and taking notes and debriefing me afterward. I guess the management hasn't much faith in their notes. But it will just be a couple of days and the stay in Tokyo won't be stressful. I'll be all rested up for you. Perhaps I'll even have my hair done.

While she chattered, I was thinking about her safety. Feng would have her covered in Hong Kong—I hoped that the length of her stay wouldn't be a problem for his friends—but we would have to take our chances in Tokyo unless it turned out that he had connections there as well. But I really couldn't, after the talk I'd just had with Feng, leave her parents, brother, sister-in-law, and their little boy without increased protection. Accordingly, apologizing for the brusque change of subject, I asked whether her father happened to be in town.

Yes, she said, funny that you should ask. He got back from Milan yesterday. Are you in the market for something from the upscale Krohn collections?

How did you guess? I laughed. I want to see whether he can get it for me wholesale.

I loved her voice. I loved her. I had never loved anyone so much or so serenely.

Feng materialized in the library, without my having rung for him, followed by Satan.

I hope I haven't kept you waiting, sir, he said. Satan and I have just had a little walk. He is ready for the night. May I bring you another whiskey?

That was exactly what I wanted. While I sipped the truly great stuff, yielding to the pleasant warmth of the liquid, Satan, probably feeling he had neglected me during dinner—he was as fond of Feng as of Heidi and me, or fonder, and often chose to sit in his crate in the kitchen watching Feng work in preference to lounging on the sofa or in an armchair wherever I happened to be—jumped into my lap with the impact of a twenty-seven-pound antitank missile, made himself comfortable, and started running through the French-bulldog scale of grunts and harrumphs. I'd so like her to come back, I thought, to lie in bed glued to her lithe and perfectly formed body, to listen to her quiet and steady breathing when she fell asleep. But I was beginning to realize that her being away for a good bit of time—it would be two weeks, I figured, before she returned—was a singular piece of luck. They might strike at me soon. It would be better if she did not witness it, if she were not in the line of fire.

Soon Satan left my lap for his usual nighttime quarters in the corner of the sofa. I gave him a good-night scratch on the head, turned out the lights, and went into my study intending to send Heidi a cheerful email, garnished with an emoji or two. My voice when we spoke, I feared, had betrayed the disappointment I felt. I opened my MacBook to Top Sites and, before I could click on Gmail, the screen went momentarily black. I tapped the space bar, whereupon a king cobra appeared, and the voice of someone educated, an American who'd picked up, along the way, a bit of an accent that wasn't exactly British, addressed me:

> Greetings, Dana! Pay attention. This time it's the boss speaking to you. Presently, a TV screen will appear. A picture is worth a thousand words. When you click on Play, which I urge you to do, you will view a video of the highlights of the execution of your Judas friend Lathrop and his wife. Such dreadful suffering! Ask yourself what may be in store for you and your lesbian Jewish slut. Good night and sweet dreams!

As though hypnotized, I did what he said. It was a high-quality video with good sound. I don't know how long I watched before I realized I could no longer bear it. There was the usual pause symbol: two vertical bars. I clicked on it. In place of the video, a new writing appeared on the TV screen, in fancy engraver's script:

You have just viewed the Flaying of Judas.

I understood that I shouldn't erase this message or the snake, or the voice or the video, even if I knew how. There was a yellow dot in the top-left corner of my screen. I clicked on it. My screen returned to Top Sites; down at the bottom of my screen there was a new icon. A green king cobra on a black background.

IV

restarted my computer, as though that would exorcise it, and then shut it down. The machine seemed hateful to me. I sent an email to Heidi from my iPhone, having worked hard to make it cheerful and attaching emoji flowers and hearts. It was half past eleven. I was very tired but knew I wouldn't be able to fall asleep. Another Oban 18? Several shots would be needed to knock me out. To hell with it. Why waste a great whiskey? I had a supply of Ambien in my medicine cabinet dating back to my sojourn at Walter Reed Army Medical Center. The stuff was loathsome, but at least it gave you five hours of solid sleep. Just right, if I was going for my usual run in the park at five-thirty.

I awoke feeling pretty awful just before the alarm clock rang, put on my running clothes, slipped the switchblade into the pocket of my sweatshirt, and, something I had never done before, decided to carry my .45. Nothing is less chic than a gun under your running clothes, unless you work for the Secret Service and also wear dark glasses and earbuds, but I wasn't going to worry about that. If the boss—no, from now on so far as I was concerned he was the Monster—sent someone to fuck with me, I'd shoot him. Unsporting but efficient. Krav Maga, the mainstay of the Israeli Defense Forces, and my knife would wait for another day, when my mood was less sour. Satan was snoring gently in his corner of the library sofa. Good dog! His day began at eight. But the ever-watchful Feng was waiting for me at the door, polite disapproval suffusing his face.

Have a safe run, sir, he offered. Breakfast will be waiting.

Neither an elevator man nor a doorman was on duty at that hour. The front door was unlocked by Emil, the night man, a garrulous Irishman of Falstaffian girth I particularly liked and who had become Satan's best buddy. He commented on the beauty of the morning, so perfect for a run in the park. Heading north, sir? I nodded agreement, crossed the avenue, and made for the Seventy-Ninth Street entrance. Heading north, sir! Dollars to doughnuts, Emil whipped out his cell phone the moment I turned my back and clued in some lowlife son of a bitch who was paying him to keep tabs on me: Hey, this is Emil. The asshole is off on his run. Yeah, uptown.

I entered the park, and for a moment considered heading south, against the traffic, just to be perverse and, with any luck, get good old Emil in trouble. But there was no point. If it were done when 'tis done, then 'twere well it were done quickly. How much longer was I supposed to waste my time on these hoods? Dealer's choice—killer's choice. Let's do it! I call and raise you!

Emil was right. A perfect morning, indeed, cool, with a

cloudless sky, and the sun just rising behind the buildings lining Fifth Avenue. No wonder the East Drive was anything but deserted. Serious runners, a good many younger than I, were thundering due north. I spotted an interval between two packs, jumped in starting slow, picked up speed, and was glad to note that, even after an Ambien night, they weren't outpacing me. Not yet. And not an orangutan in a ski mask in sight, and no tail. Hey, I could run and think.

What were my obligations to the Westchester D.A.'s office and the FBI? I had as much as agreed to report if anything new came up—the invasion of my laptop, the monstrous video, and the threats directed at Heidi and me surely fit that definition—but what if I didn't report or if I delayed? I didn't want the cops moving in and trying to build a wall around me, but I didn't want to get indicted for obstructing justice or for some other bullshit reason either. The cops weren't going to catch the Monster and his boys, and I was not sure they could or would keep me and Heidi and her family safe while we led normal lives. And how long could this sort of "witness protection" last? Real safety lay in my killing whomever the Monster sent and, although it seemed far-fetched, if luck was with me, killing the Monster too. That meant letting them have a go at me as many times as it would take for me to strike back. Crazy? Perhaps, but Abner had tried hard to take me out, and he and every one of the hit men he sent after me were dead. This was different, because Heidi was under threat, and her safety had to come first. I couldn't expose her to harm. The Krohn security people were first-rate, Martin Sweeney had assured me. But were the retired Mossad and special-agent types as good a repellent as the cops? Clearly, I had to consult Heidi and her father. I also needed legal advice about my duties to the D.A. and the FBI. Would Moses Cohen, my terrific Orthodox Jewish trusts and estates lawyer, know enough to give it? He seems to know a lot, I told myself. If this is out of his range, he'll get help.

It occurred to me by the time I'd reached East Ninety-Sixth Street that this was as good a time as any to revisit the Ravine, the scene of one of my more brilliant encounters with Abner's thugs. Does history really repeat itself as farce? Eager to find out, I continued north for about half a mile and cut west. The Ravine and the waterfall were as enchanting as ever. With a touch of disappointment, I noted that no one was tailing me as I headed toward West One Hundred Third Street. Hello! Was this the farcical element? My path was suddenly barred by two burly types carrying nail-studded cudgels who'd appeared from nowhere. Nowhere couldn't be right. More likely they had been crouching behind a clump of bushes. Whoever sent them had made an intelligent study of my exploits and habits and had guessed correctly that the Monster's message would send me to this particular spot like a homing pigeon. He also had a sense of humor. Stuck-up asshole Dana, we'll show him. But did he remember that the previous encounter had ended badly for Abner's boy? Perhaps he didn't care. Hit men are like Kleenex tissues: disposable. These fellows, almost as tall as I but heavier and very unsmiling, had made no effort to look like early morning Yuppie runners. They wore the uniform of two-bit hoods: black sweatshirts, black jeans, black combat boots laced only halfway up, and biker gloves.

Let's beat the shit out of this guy, said the one on my right, and spat a huge glob of phlegm.

Yeah, give it to him! chimed in the other.

Unlike Abner's thugs, these fellows were homegrown. He'd gotten me accustomed to rich Slavic accents and diction. This was Harlem or the equivalent.

One on each side, they closed in. I've often wished that heaven would rain blessings on my Krav Maga trainer, Wolf, but never more fervently than that morning. I ducked under the raised arm of the fellow on my left and stuck the switchblade into his side. Deep enough, I hoped, to pierce the lung. He let out a scream and started hugging himself, which is a semi-reflexive reaction to that kind of wound. The other guy circled around and went into a crouch, swaying from side to side, ready to rush me. He was smart. This was the way to deal with my knife.

But he didn't stand a chance. Shifting the switchblade to my left hand, I drew the .45 from the shoulder holster and barked, using my best Marine Corps Infantry command voice, You guys want to die? You, wise guy, drop that stick. Both of you, sit. Cross-legged. Hands on top of your heads.

The wounded fellow was groaning, and they both hesitated, but only for a brief moment.

Move it, I said, or I'll shoot to kill. All right, and now talk! Who sent you?

Nobody, replied the one I'd wounded. Man, I need help. Get me help.

There was red-colored saliva on his lips. He was right; he needed an ambulance.

And you, I addressed the other guy, are you going to talk?

Ain't no one sent us, he answered. We wanted to rob you, man.

That was bullshit, but there was no way I was going to get the truth out of them short of letting the other fellow keep bleeding and perhaps cracking this guy's kneecap. Fuck it! What they knew wasn't worth shit.

All right, I said, I'm calling 911 and I'll stay with you until the cops get here. Sit still and don't move.

The police cruiser and an ambulance arrived within minutes. I rode to the West One Hundredth Street precinct in the back seat of the cruiser, alongside the handcuffed thug I hadn't cut. The medics took away the other guy. We were the first clients at the station that morning, and taking down my statement took no time. I assured the duty sergeant that I'd be available if the D.A. wanted me—the circle of my acquaintances among prosecutors was apparently going to be once again enlarged—hailed a cab on Broadway, and asked to be driven home. Yes, the idea that I might run to Fifth Avenue and Eighty-Second Street did cross my mind, but I was sane enough to reject it. Instead I called Feng from the cab and told him I was on the way. Nothing shook my conviction as I reviewed the events at the Ravine that these punks were hired hands on a mission. Real robbers don't look for customers in that remote corner of the park at six-thirty in the morning.

Feng greeted me at the door with a politely blank expression.

A long run, sir, he observed. Thank you for telephoning. Will you shower and change before breakfast?

Not this once, I answered. Could I eat in the kitchen? I'm starved.

Certainly, sir. Shall I put the telephone receiver on the table? Mr. Prentice telephoned half an hour ago. He expects your call.

Of course, I replied.

No question about it. At Fifth Avenue, I was in the doghouse. I downed my orange juice and one cup of steaming coffee. Seated on the floor on my left, Satan was giving me a puzzled look that meant: What's wrong with you this morning, why is the service so lousy? I've been waiting and waiting. It was time for his banana, and I was seriously late presenting it to him. As every morning, Feng, who doted on Satan as much as I, had prepared it on a little plate placed next to mine. I peeled the banana, cut half of it into fruit-salad-thickness slices, and, one by one, fed them to the Frenchie. Both he and Feng began to look less cross. That's all for this morning, I told the Frenchie, gave him a pat on the head, and called Scott on his private cell phone.

I knew that he put it on Do Not Disturb when he couldn't talk freely, and in those cases got back to me later. This time he answered right away. Ever discreet Feng was about to withdraw. I gestured for him to stay and told Scott that I seemed to be in ever-deeper shit. Feng hadn't heard what I was about to say, and if I put us on the loudspeaker I wouldn't have to go over the same ground twice. Would he mind?

No problem, he replied, whereupon I related the previous evening's invasion of my computer, the video of the murders, the Monster's message to me, and my morning run. He kept interrupting with his signature low whistles, but I just plugged on, stopping only with my taxi ride home.

Holy shit! Have you really finished? asked Scott.

Yup. The floor is yours and Feng's.

All right, Scott said, I'll go first. Congratulations on keeping your cool and not killing those thugs. The last thing you need is trouble with the law over homicide. It would be interesting to know whether they'd been sent to beat you to death or just maim you. I sort of think the latter. Now some good news: my colleague who deals with the Bureau perked right up when I mentioned Joe Edwards, the special agent you met in White Plains. According to him, Edwards is first-rate: well educated—law degree from Notre Dame—very bright, and sophisticated. And a hell of a nice guy. Married to a black woman working for the Queens D.A. They have one child. A toddler. The guy has a big heart.

You're really sold on this guy. Something tells me, or I've read, that the FBI is Trumpland. I'm not at all sure how this paragon is going to take to me.

Jack, you may be right as a general matter. Some people would say that about the Agency as well. It doesn't matter. This guy has his big heart in the right place, and, so far as experience is concerned, it's the perfect fit. He's the point man in New York on organized crime, including international aspects. I guarantee you'll like him. My colleague is filling him in on your and my relationship, and he'll most likely call you this morning. Don't put him off. He should also meet Feng. Listen carefully to Edwards's advice, and for Christ's sake, try to stay alive!

Special Agent Joseph X. Edwards called moments after I hung up with Scott and came over a couple of hours later. I hadn't paid attention to his appearance in White Plains: he was a brawnier version of Dick Tracy as played by Warren Beatty. In view of what Scott had told me about him, I wasn't going to worry about his politics. He addressed me as Captain, explaining that he'd boned up on my background.

That was years ago, I told him. Now I'm a civilian. Please call me Jack, and allow me to call you Joe, if that's all right under the Bureau's rules.

I'd be honored, sir, if you called me Joe, but once a marine, always a marine. I deployed to Anbar in 2006, with the Second Division, took reserve status in 2010. I thought I was lucky to be in one piece.

You're damn right, if you were there for Ramadi.

I was, sir. It's not something I'll ever forget.

He went on to explain that he'd enlisted right after Boston College, didn't apply to officer-candidate school, and didn't reenlist. The way the war was going, five years of active duty were more than enough. The G.I. Bill of Rights and the Notre

Dame financial-aid program helped him make it through law school without debt. And, he concluded, he was doing the work he'd always wanted to do.

He asked me to recount once again the story of my contacts with the Monster, from the first nighttime telephone call, explaining that hearing it directly from me might allow him to pick up significant details that had been otherwise missed.

I did as I was told and asked whether he'd learned anything new.

He shook his head and asked to take a look at my laptop. The video was still there.

That's weird, he said. They have total control of your laptop, so they could have pulled the video. It means to me, sir, that they want other people to see it too.

He clicked on the Play icon and watched—longer than I had thought possible.

Real sadists, sick, sick, and dangerous, he spat out. Manson? Sharon Tate? This is much, much worse. Our technicians will need to download this thing. The question I have to ask you, sir, is what you want to do about your computer.

I'm not sure, Joe, that I understand the question or that I really understand what has happened to my laptop. As you can imagine, it's where I work. I write my books on it. I do know, of course, that the computer has been hacked and presumably all my passwords are compromised. That's about the extent of my knowledge, and I'm afraid you have to help me work through the problem.

All right, sir. I'm going to oversimplify. First, as I said, these bastards have complete control of your machine. How did they do it? By installing a rootkit in it—a collection of malware—that lets them put in additional software. Most likely it was done through phishing—getting you to click on an innocent-looking link that appears in what seems like an email from a trusted source but is in reality a phony. For instance, a fake message from the fraud-detection unit of one of your credit cards. Or a phony advertisement for a product that interests you. There are other methods, such as hiding a virus on a perfectly legitimate website that you visit. It will probably surprise you that there are viruses hidden in certain pages of *The New York Times* and *The Wall Street Journal.* Not always the same. You open the page, let's say an article on a historical figure, really any article, and you catch the virus. The security companies try to keep up. If you've downloaded one of their protection systems, you'll receive update patches, but it's almost impossible to keep up with the hackers. They now send zero viruses. Those arrive in the morning and they've done their work by the time the patch becomes available. Bottom line, right now the computer belongs to the bastard who's sending you this stuff as much as to you. The viruses are hidden deep in the operating system. We can clean the hard drive. But if we do that, we'll cut off the channel he uses to communicate with you.

We don't want to do that, I said. I'm sure he'd find another method, but it could be even worse.

I agree with you.

I think I know the answer but let me ask the question anyway: Would the bastard, as you call him, know the computer has been cleaned?

Most certainly. Because he could no longer control it.

All right, here is another subject that's very important to me. I'm writing a book. It's in my computer, in Word. I don't print anything out at this stage. There are also successive drafts in Word that I've saved and sent to a special Gmail account I use only for that purpose. Whatever is in Word on the computer, he can manipulate. Read it? Insert stuff into my text?

Absolutely.

Is there some way my book and my notes can be cleaned?

Joe was too polite to shrug his shoulders.

In theory, yes, he said, but it's extremely unlikely there are viruses in your text, although what you've written may have been maliciously doctored. Still, if you buy a new computer and keep it clean, which is what I recommend, you'd be taking an unnecessary risk if you transfer to it any—I mean any—files from the old computer.

In that case, what do you think I should do? I asked.

There is a simple low-tech solution: you will print your book and any notes and any other material you have stored in your present computer that you want to keep, and then input it all into the new machine. I know it's a pain, sir, but it's safe and it will work.

Got it, I replied. In the end retyping what I've written may be good for my book. Now here's the next question. And photos?

I'll speak to one of our specialists. My simple solution once again is print. Print the ones you want. Let the others stay on your machine. But I may be able to get back with more sophisticated advice.

What about my Gmail accounts?

Unless you log off after every use of the accounts, he now has control of them. By now he probably knows all your passwords, either because they're stored on your computer or because he's been able to follow the keystrokes when you log on. When you get your new machine, you will want to create a whole new set of passwords and protect them by logging off each time you finish doing whatever you're doing: checking your bank balance, paying bills, shopping online, reading and sending emails—whatever. And you should tell your bank and credit-card companies that you have a hacking problem and that your current passwords are no longer valid.

I kind of doubt this guy is interested in my money, I replied, but I will.

You can't be sure. He's a fucking—excuse me—sadist, and he may want to screw you in ways that won't matter to him but will cause you damage or will tie you up in knots.

Understood, I said. I'll get a new laptop this afternoon. Now what about my present laptop? If you study it, can you determine where this bastard's messages come from?

Zero likelihood, sir. The rootkit his people have installed wouldn't have been sent from any computer associated with them. They'll have used other computers they got control of—possibly very many of them—that belong, saving your reverence, to other suckers just like you. So if we're able to trace anything they do in relation to your computer to a

source, that source will be to one of those hacked computers. That being said, we'll look. We'll also—I assume you don't
mind—tap into your present computer so we can study traffic
coming into it in real time. But if these people are as skilled
as they seem to be, they will still escape.

Right, I said, feeling tired and discouraged. But wait a minute. All these Russian and Chinese and other known hackers.
Specialists do figure out who they are. Maybe not the person,
but the organization. That's what the *Times* tells me. Then
what about me?

Roughly, the difference is that those hackers, who have
hacked into our government or into Sony or into the DNC
or have been fucking—excuse me, sir—with computers
worldwide asking for ransom, were at it a long time on those
systems, and left what you might call signature traces. We'll
study your laptop. But I will be truly surprised if we find anything like that.

And what about my cell phone? It's synced with my computer? Does that mean that the son of a bitch has control of
it as well?

Not if your phone hasn't gone missing.

You mean if I haven't lost it?

Something like that. If there hasn't been a time when
someone could install a program on it. If there was, you could
have a jailbreak, a case of their overriding your iPhone's
software and installing their own apps or software without
Apple's approval. Otherwise, the only software that can
be run on your iPhone is apps downloaded from the Apple
App Store, which are examined and approved by Apple. The

amazing thing is that even if you opened a phishing email on your iPhone, the operating system wouldn't let you download or run a virus. It's a very, very closed system. That doesn't mean they haven't found a way of listening to your phone calls. They may well have. You will want to consider getting a burner for calls you really want to keep private.

Ah, yes. I nodded. I know about burners.

Joe looked at me carefully and said, I realize I've given you a headache with this stuff. Bottom line: get yourself a new computer for your literary work, for emails you don't want these bastards to read, and for doing your banking and credit-card transactions. Don't transfer anything from the old machine onto it. Keep the old machine, in order to receive messages from the boss, even though he may get tired of that game. If you have questions about any of this computer stuff, or anything else, call me. I'm there for you twenty-four seven. Would it be all right if I spoke to Feng now? After that, let's discuss how to catch those bastards and keep you alive.

I sneaked into the pantry and poured myself a double or triple bourbon and sipped it and read the *Times* on my poor infected computer while they talked. Trump, Trump, Trump. I was tired of reading and hearing about him. He was making me depressed and sick. He was making a majority of other Americans depressed and sick, I was sure of that, and good people everywhere, worldwide.

Feng is first-rate, Joe declared when he returned from their nearly hour-long conference in the kitchen. Knows police work and is completely devoted to you. You're lucky, sir, to have him working for you. He understands the nature of the grave dangers you face. It also happens that he is very calm about it. You've really won his friendship.

I agree with all that, was my reply. Will you join me in a drink?

Not while I'm on duty, sir, but thank you very much. Feng gave me a very good cup of coffee in the kitchen and some pound cake he baked.

I'm glad of that, I said. So now will you tell me what you are doing to catch this son of a bitch and his gangsters?

All the usual stuff. I don't mind telling you that it's been one dry hole after another. But we've only had a couple of days. Sometimes one gets lucky. We're examining the telephone traffic of a whole bunch of people. Eventually, the bastards will get clumsy or unlucky. Confidentially, sir, I too think our big chance may be their next move against you. We need to take advantage of it, and at the same time we need to make sure you're all right.

You mean police protection? Once I have it, there will never be such a move, unless they get a sniper to shoot me in the street or something like it. They won't want to tangle with a bunch of cops. If you want to catch them through me, you need to let them make that move.

It won't be that sort of protection. The way we'll keep an eye on you, even you won't know we're doing it. We'll be in the wings, that's all. Very discreet, but I hope effective.

And what about my friend, Miss Heidi Krohn? Her family business has a full-blown security service, but I'm more concerned about her than about myself.

When she's with you it will be the same deal, and it will be in addition to whatever else she has. I'll check at the office, but I don't think we can commit to protecting her family or even protecting her twenty-four seven wherever she goes and whatever she's doing. I hope you'll understand the problem.

I do understand, I answered, but that problem is a huge problem for me. My biggest source of worry and vulnerability.

Yes, sir. I will check, and of course the situation could change.

All right, I continued, what about the Westchester D.A.? Do I have to go up there and tell his people everything I've told you, or will you fill him in?

We'll take care of it. If he needs anything more, he'll let you know. But we'd appreciate it if you'd let me know if anything new comes up. Here is all my contact information. Once again: you should feel free to call anytime, day or night.

As I was seeing him out the front door, Joe said, I've remembered something I should check. Can we take one more look at your computer?

I told him the password, which he wrote in his notebook, and asked him to sit down in my desk chair and poke around as much as he liked.

It's the video, he said, I wanted to make sure it was still on your hard drive and it is. We need to copy it so it can be examined. Could one of our technicians come over in a couple of hours?

Certainly, I said. Either I or Feng will be here.

Good. And could we borrow the laptop for the night, say

pick it up tonight at eleven and return it tomorrow morning at eight, so we can give it a thorough going-over?

Certainly, I said. If I need to read my emails or send an email, I'll use my phone.

I was about to close the cover of the laptop when the screen went black, exactly as it did before the first message from the boss. The same image of a cobra appeared, followed by writing:

You have no brains and no luck. I don't know when or how I will kill you, or even whether I'll kill you. But you will curse the day you were born, and the night it was said there is a man-child conceived.

V

Pretentious son of a bitch, I said.

You're taking this very calmly, sir, observed Joe.

What do you expect? I answered crossly. I didn't go looking for this Monster. He isn't sure whether he wants to draw and quarter me or just kill me or perhaps both! That's nice. I'd like to say that I'll do all I can to kill him first, but I've no idea how to go about it. No idea about who he might be. This mafioso stuff—how this is a vendetta to avenge Abner Brown—I'm not sure I believe it, and anyway it doesn't tell me how to get at him. You and your colleagues don't have a clue either. By the way, will this SOB know when you're somehow plugged in to my computer and reading his messages? If that's the case, please don't plug in. I wouldn't want to do anything to inhibit the flow of this shit.

Fair point, sir. I will strongly recommend we follow your wishes.

Thanks!

I wasn't about to tell Joe, but it had also occurred to me

that if he or his colleagues were following the Monster's messages in real time they might thwart whatever he intended to try next. Real action, and not just talking rubbish. I was beginning to want him to strike. Strike at me. There was no other way to end this nightmare.

Joe had seen right through me.

I guess, sir, he added with a grin, that you're not keen on our interfering with his next move. That's just a thought that occurred to me, so I'll keep it to myself. But please don't forget that our mission comes in two parts: catching those bastards and keeping you out of trouble.

He thought I was cool. That was nice. Little did he know what was going on inside me. Or perhaps he did. Perhaps everyone did.

Feng relented. He didn't protest when I told him, after Joe had left, that I was taking Satan out for his noon walk around the block. The little beast seemed content to see me resume my duties. Since French bulldogs are born with just a little stub of a corkscrew in place of a tail, he couldn't wag it. But he rewarded me by relieving himself expeditiously beside the tree on Eighty-Second Street, between Fifth and Madison, to which I had guided him. You're a good boy, a very good boy, I told him as I picked up the huge mess with a baggie I extracted from the back pocket of my trousers. Bending down to do so, I realized what a ridiculously easy target I presented: a man who has something like a price on his head stooping and trying hard with one hand to remove every trace of dog shit from the sidewalk—a task that demands concentration if you're as civic minded as I—and with the other hand holding the lead at the end of which were twenty-seven pounds of muscle and bone absolutely determined, now that his business was done, to hit the road. There was no way I could ward off the blow of a blackjack or the thrust of a knife. Once more, Feng was right.

I forbore telling him so when Satan and I got back to the apartment. No matter how many times his advice was right on target, I had to preserve some semblance of autonomy! Instead, so as to leave no doubt about my independence, I told him I was going out to lunch at my club. Then I'd see Heidi's father, if he was free, and since his office happened to be in the same building as Apple's Fifth Avenue store, I'd most likely stop there and buy a new laptop.

Provided I'm still alive! I added.

Feng replied, Very good, sir, and didn't so much as smile.

The guy has no sense of humor, I said to myself, and decided to take the subway from Seventy-Seventh Street and Lexington to Grand Central and walk from there to the club. That was, as I knew well, a stupid thing to do. Nothing is easier than to push someone under an arriving train—that was what Abner Brown's hit man Slobo did to my uncle Harry's secretary—and it's a hell of a way to die. So I kept my eyes peeled on my way to the subway station, waited for the number 6 train away from the edge of the platform, as the MTA monotonously recommends, and, bolt upright and alert, observed everything within sight or hearing. There was nothing out of the way to report, no violation of general or special orders: just the usual New York stew of young and old, sexy and repulsive, with a few bums thrown in for added spice. A killer needs space for his work. I dashed into the most crowded car and elbowed my way into the middle of a Puerto Rican family of six. They were to be my human shield. I got out of the car like a human torpedo. If you know Grand Central, getting around the terminal is simple. I zoomed through that magnificent soaring space, past overweight and undertrained National Guard sentries and tourists taking selfies, emerged on Vanderbilt Avenue, and headed for the club. My uncle Harry had been a member of this grand institution, as had Simon Lathrop, who put me up for membership after Harry's death and saw to my rapid admission.

You're the youngest member here, my boy, he told me after I'd been elected. I'm pleased as punch. The club needs new blood.

Blood. As in the pools of gore on the bed and on the floor, where Jennie and he were butchered.

I had never been to the club alone. Before he was murdered, I'd only gone there to lunch with Harry and later, even after I'd been elected, only with Simon. Simon had introduced me punctiliously to the club's manager, accountants, hall porters, and barmen and waiters as the noted novelist and genuine war hero who was, moreover, the late Mr. Harry Dana's nephew. One of the many endearing qualities of the club's personnel is their courtesy and unfailing memory for faces and names. They had all offered me their condolences on account of Harry as soon as I became a member—such a lovely gentleman, always so thoughtful and kind—and now, knowing of my friendship with Simon, they told me how sorry and shocked they were and summoned memories of him as the great connoisseur of good food and fine wines. And poor Mrs. Lathrop! Such a fine lady! Yes, yes, I agreed, a terrible loss, one with which I had not yet come to terms. Perhaps I never will, I added.

Not wanting to drink at the bar, I went straight up to the nearly empty members' dining room. The ceiling would not have fallen in, I suppose, if I had sat down alone at one of the tables for two, but that would have been aggressively contrary to club custom. Neither Harry nor Simon would have approved. Accordingly, I overcame my reluctance and sat down, next to an aged gentleman, at the long table which is where members who are alone are supposed to lunch or dine. Across from us were three equally ancient types, also unknown to me. Still in accordance with club custom, we did not introduce ourselves. Instead, I greeted them with a cheerful good morning, which was appropriately reciprocated, whereupon the quartet of ancients resumed their discussion of the firing of Jim Comey. They had vivid recollections of Nixon's Saturday Night Massacre and thought the country was heading for a similar train wreck. I filled out my lunch and bar chits: chicken salad and a glass of Pouilly-Fumé. As I later ordered a double espresso and munched on a macaroon, my neighbors' conversation veered to problems with one's dentist and, specifically, the fix one was in when the dentist one has been with forever decides to retire. Harmless chitchat, a bulwark against loneliness and sadness. Their world was not my world. Oh yes, I guess I understood that their polite good cheer might be a façade behind which hid many ills: sickness afflicting people about whom they care more than about themselves, anxiety about their children's vulnerabilities and failures, the bitterness of body and soul falling asunder. But, surely, they faced nothing and no one so terrifyingly malign as the Monster.

You seem lost in a reverie, kindly observed the octogenarian on my left. A happy reverie, I hope! By the way, don't I recognize your face from book jackets and articles about your books?

It's possible, I replied. The book-jacket photo is a pretty good likeness. You'll have to excuse me, though. I've just realized that I am on the verge of missing an appointment.

That was a lie. I hadn't called Heidi's father and thought I should give him another half hour to get back from lunch, but I couldn't bear the prospect of a discussion, in which my other neighbors would surely join, of my literary production. I needed to be alone with the Monster.

There was a back room into which I thought my lunch companions were unlikely to venture. As I expected, it was deserted. I sank into an armchair facing away from the door and closed my eyes. So much the better if whoever looked in concluded I was catching a postprandial snooze. A project that made me ashamed was irresistibly taking shape in my mind: it was to flee. If I managed to persuade Heidi to come with me, we could, at least for a time, leave behind not only the Monster and his works but also the forces of order with whom I was of necessity allied. Joe Edwards, the FBI, Captain Morrison, D.A. Curley—whoever else marching under the banner of law and order cared to join the parade.

During my first summer vacation from prep school, my parents rented in Senlis, a small town about an hour north from Paris, an eighteenth-century hunting lodge belonging to a widowed French countess who used it only during the open season on roe deer. The main house, the adjoining guardian's cottage, and the garden had the peculiarity of being enclosed by high walls. It was a singularly secure place, one that Feng and I could certainly defend if the Monster succeeded in finding us, something that I would make as difficult as possible. There was a swimming pool within the walls. Even if the summer turned out to be hot, one could find refreshment in it, and for all I knew Madame de Lorches had put in air-conditioning. The trails in the forest of Chantilly shaded by a canopy of old trees were exquisitely well maintained, so different from the woods between Sag Harbor and Bridgehampton, where if a tree fell it remained until termites had turned it into sawdust and, as soon as the weather turned warm, the danger of tick and chigger attacks made me give up walking there with Satan. Another resource was a distinctly unfashionable club, midway between Senlis and Chantilly, where Madame de Lorches had gotten us a summer membership. Heidi was a strong swimmer. She might like its Olympic-size swimming pool. I couldn't remember whether the horses we rode that summer were provided by the club or by a commercial stable, but they were lively and clean, perfect for the forest trails. How I would reconcile using the club, riding or hiking in the forest, and other such activities with our need for security was a puzzle I would have to solve. Feng's not knowing any French was a problem, but I would take him to Senlis, introduce him to the local butcher and grocer, and he could do his shopping armed with a list I'd write out in French.

Armed. That could be a much bigger problem. Was there any way Feng or I could bring our handguns to France? Possibly the FBI could arrange it, but that would mean taking Joe Edwards into my confidence. That was not part of my plan, but I liked the guy and thought that, if necessary, I could bring him on board. Otherwise, I could surely buy a pair of shotguns. Perhaps also big-game-hunting rifles. That's where the daydream ended. The image of Feng and me, shotgun or elephant rifle at the ready, standing guard on the ramparts of Madame de Lorches's house, was too preposterous. A house that for all I knew Madame de Lorches wasn't renting or had sold or, if she was dead, which given her age did not seem unlikely, had passed to her heirs. And who might they be? All right, everybody is entitled to a daydream or two. That was not a problem. Something else was: the possibility that I had lost my nerve, that the desire to leave the Monster behind me and run away to the France of my boyhood was the prelude to cowardice in the face of the enemy. Let me die, I thought, before I find myself guilty of that sin.

I shook off these thoughts. From the telephone booth downstairs, I called Heidi's father. He did not conceal his surprise when I asked whether I could see him at his office, preferably that same afternoon.

Certainly, Jack, he said, certainly. Is there a problem? Helen—that was the name of Heidi's mother—spoke with Heidi yesterday evening, just before going to bed, and she said Heidi was very pleased with herself. Winning her arbitration, being fêted by the client, and so forth.

That's what she told me too, I answered, but I've something to discuss that's too complicated to explain on the telephone. That's why, if you have a half hour . . .

Of course, of course, dear boy. Come right over and take all the time you need.

Krohn Enterprises occupied an entire very high floor of the GM Building. I shuddered at what it must cost to rent. Heidi's great-grandfather started out sewing shirts somewhere on the Lower East Side and progressed to owning a sweatshop in the West Thirties. There, other people working for him sewed and sweated. Her grandfather moved the operation to Seventh Avenue. It made fancier and fancier ready-to-wear women's clothes. And now her father, on whom I was about to call, stood at the head of an apparel and real estate empire that entitled him to an honorable perch on Bloomberg's list of the four hundred richest billionaires in the world. The secretary who ushered me into the private conference room adjoining his office—gray hair pinned in a bun, pearls, ivory silk blouse, black knee-length skirt, and black pumps—could have stepped out from a 1950s movie. Introducing herself as Miss Fish, she murmured, Welcome, Mr. Dana, very welcome. I've heard so much about you and, of course, I've read your books. Mr. Krohn is on the telephone and will join you as soon as possible. May I offer you coffee or tea?

I asked for tea and fell to contemplating the view that, on this very clear day, stretched to the Statue of Liberty and beyond. It was interrupted by the simultaneous arrival of Mr. Krohn and the tea. He guided me to his office and asked me to sit down on one of the armchairs on the visitor's side of his huge desk covered with neat stacks of documents.

He sank into the other one and, dispensing with preliminaries, said, Jack, is there a problem? I'm delighted to see you, but somehow your call has made me feel something's wrong. Please tell me.

I'll be blunt, Mr. Krohn, I replied. I think I have already brought you and Mrs. Krohn a ton of worries and troubles, and I'm not sure that I've even begun to apologize for it. That man who tried to run Heidi off the road—I think you've figured it out, or perhaps Heidi told you, that was a case of mistaken identity. Heidi was driving my car, and when he rammed it he thought he was going to kill me. Fortunately, the seat belt and the airbags worked as they should; Heidi was only shaken up, but it was a close call. And now I may be causing you even more worries.

Jack, he broke in. First of all, please call me Jon. And please call Helen by her first name too. Enough with the Mr.-and-Mrs. stuff. Second, you've brought incredible joy into our lives. Don't you know that? Heidi hasn't been so happy since she was a little girl. You're good for her. We're beginning to hope, Helen and I, that you and she will one day soon become a family! What do you think of that?

Only that I love her more than I've ever loved anybody, I told him. I do think that things are going well between us. But you and Mrs. Krohn, I mean Helen, know better than anyone that this is a complicated subject for Heidi. She's got to have space. She mustn't be rushed or pushed. But I am hers, on whatever basis she wants me, and for however long she'll keep me. Forever would be best. Now I really have to tell you why I needed to see you so urgently.

The mogul wiped tears from his eyes with his silk breast-pocket square and nodded.

All right, I said. This isn't easy. You've read about the murder in Westchester of Simon Lathrop and his wife. Simon had been my uncle Harry Dana's best friend, and he befriended me. In a small way he helped when I looked for evidence of the criminal behavior of many of Abner Brown's businesses. He was also instrumental in forcing the departure of two partners from his and Uncle Harry's firm, one of whom was the firm's chairman at the time. They had in effect become Brown's henchmen.

All right, I said again, catching my breath. While the Lathrops were being murdered, I received a phone call. The caller said the boss wants you to hear your friends scream—or something to that effect. My computer has been hacked, not for the usual purposes, such as emptying my bank account, but to send me astonishing and horrifying messages that threaten me and—here is the worst part—that also threaten Heidi. In vile language.

Jack, cried Jonathan, this is for the police! For the FBI! This is organized crime! I know the commissioner and I know the director—of course, poor Jim Comey has been fired, but I'll get through to his deputy. I'll get them on the line right now.

The FBI is already on the case, I told him, and I suppose

the New York police as well. The Westchester D.A. was going to be in touch with all the right people. Anyway, the special agent with whom I'm dealing has told me that they'll be watching over me and over Heidi when she is with me. He wasn't sure that the Bureau would provide the same sort of protection for Heidi when she is off on her own, or for you or Helen and the rest of your family. Not for the time being. It's a question of resources, I guess. However that works out, it's a complicated business, since both Heidi and I want to go on leading normal lives. In Heidi's case there is the added complication that she'll be in Hong Kong till the end of next week and then she'll be in Tokyo for a few days. My housekeeper, Feng, is a former special-unit Hong Kong policeman and he has arranged for protection over there by a couple of his friends, very discreet protection so that she won't be aware of it. I don't want her to refuse protection or freak out and do less than her very best in the arbitration. I have one hundred percent confidence in everything Feng says and does. But that leaves Tokyo uncovered. By the way, I haven't told Heidi any of this. She's got to keep her mind on her case.

Mr. Krohn had been nodding energetically.

You're right. This is not the time to tell her, and I won't say a word to Helen. Let's leave Hong Kong to Feng's friends. My security people will figure out what to do in Tokyo. Probably get someone to check into her hotel and basically stand guard outside when she's in the room and get some of our other people to shadow her. I'll get that started. And once she comes back, and you've told her everything, we'll have our security watch over her. And over you, dear boy, if you will allow me. And I am going to call the deputy director. This is too serious to be left to a special agent.

Thank you, I replied. May I ask that when you speak to the deputy you tell him specifically that I think very highly of Agent Joe Edwards, with whom I've been in contact?

Count on it. I won't forget.

He took a notepad out of his pocket and wrote on it.

Joe Edwards, he repeated, Special Agent Joe Edwards. Now something else. So far as I'm concerned, you're like a son-in-law to me. I hope someday you will be that officially. So please don't take unnecessary risks and stay alive. For Heidi!

I promise I will, I replied. Apropos of that, what with FBI protection or surveillance, and Feng's and my own ability to take care of ourselves, I don't think I personally need the extra layer from Krohn security. Heidi's case is different. But I'm very grateful.

All right, all right, let's see how things develop. There is something else I want to tell you about Heidi. You know she has one brother. Mike. Michael. You've met him and his new wife. That's number three, by the way. Fortunately, there were no children with number one or number two. Now he has a little boy. Little Jonjon—they named him for me—is a very cute fellow. I hope they'll bring him up well. Anyway, this is just a preface. Mike has been a big disappointment to me. He's frivolous and weak and conceited. Not a good combination for running my company. My great hope is that I can get him to stand aside without acrimony and that, once this has been accomplished, Heidi will join me here as my right hand and my successor. You see how much she means to me—and not only because she's my only daughter, or because she's super bright, or because she's good as gold but tough, or because she's beautiful. She's the apple of my eye. So stay alive and take good care of her. I would die of grief if any harm came to her.

Once again, I said, I promise. That's the way I feel about her too.

He rose out of his armchair, took me in his arms, and hugged me.

God bless you! I'll be reaching out to the deputy director.

I'd called ahead to have my new MacBook loaded with Word. It was ready. I bought a case for it and, in defiance of Feng's prescriptions, strolled home on the park side of Fifth Avenue. It was time for Satan's first evening walk when I arrived. Feng put the leash on him with a resigned air and handed it to me. As for Satan, his grunts allowed no doubt about his satisfaction. It was an uneventful outing, marked only by the little Frenchie's meeting his best friend, Winston, a black-and-white Frenchie being walked by his owner, a woman writer whose frequent contributions to *The New York Review of Books* I admire. As usual we exchanged anecdotes of Winston's and Satan's most recent exploits and agreed to try to meet the next day for a morning walk around the Great Lawn.

Back home, I told Feng that Heidi would have Krohn security protection in Tokyo and, of course, when she came home.

That's very good, sir. Will you have coffee or tea or a drink?

Thank you, Feng, nothing just now.

I couldn't resist sneaking a look at my old computer. Feng had told me that an FBI technician had appeared in the early afternoon and had spent some time with it. It was the machine on which I had written all my published books and was writing the new one, and now it had been fatally polluted. I would never work on it again. Instead, I would ask it to disgorge as much of the new book as I had written and then entrust it to the novice, the laptop I hadn't yet brought into my study. I typed in my password. My Top Sites came up. When I clicked on the cobra icon, the intruder messages were still there. Otherwise, nothing new. I couldn't bear even the thought of replaying the video of the Lathrops' agony, but something still inchoate urged me to reread the messages. I opened them and found at once what I had been looking for. These strange phrases—the execution of your Judas friend Lathrop, your Jewish slut, you have no brains and no luck—they were like an air you hear on the radio when you're not paying attention. It sounds vaguely familiar, you think it must be ballet music, but for the moment you can't place it. *Nutcracker?* You shake your head. Then the melody comes back, this time you really listen, and all at once you know: it's the dance of the little swans in *Swan Lake,* just before von Rothbart appears. Similarly, I suddenly realized what I was hearing. Abner's diction! His mixture of vulgarity and grandiloquence. Of course, it was Abner, except that, as I kept repeating, Abner was dead, dead and cremated, ashes scattered. And dead men don't post messages, through Ouija boards or otherwise. But it didn't have to be Abner's ghost.

It could be quite simply someone with a good ear for speech patterns and with a taste for the macabre as sick as Abner's.

But who?

I closed the messages and looked carefully at the cobra home page. The huge green snake was slithering. At irregular intervals it rose and looked me straight in the face, ready to strike. Previously, each time it had gone through its contortions, I was too outraged or terrified to pay the home page sufficient attention. Now I saw that there was a dim, or anyway discreet, toolbar at the top of the page, and that it included Home, which is where I was, About Us, Archive, and Contact. If I clicked on Archive, the messages and the video came up. Clicking on About Us elicited as reply:

Access Currently Denied

Let's go, I whispered to myself and clicked on Contact. The little spinning circle appeared. My laptop was working hard to open whatever lay beyond. After some seconds, a keyboard appeared and above it a box in which a message could be written.

Without stopping to consider, I wrote:

Who are you, Monster? How can I get you off my back?

A message appeared with the speed of a computer-generated reply:

Inquiries will be answered in the order they are received.

VI

I wasn't going to remain glued to my laptop screen awaiting my turn. That was no doubt what the Monster expected, but I wasn't in the mood to play along. I glanced at my watch. It was past six. No reason why I couldn't have a drink. I wanted one badly. But except for my run in the park, shortened by the eruption of the Monster's thugs, I had had no exercise, and I hadn't exercised the day before. I called the gym. My trainer, Wolf, hadn't left for the day and was willing to stay for an hour of Krav Maga if I came right over. I told Feng I was going out and reminded him that he had specifically told me I didn't need an escort to Third Avenue and back.

Quite right, sir, he answered. Have a good workout.

I was in the mood to mollify Feng, so I said I'd have dinner at home if he could take Satan out for his evening walk and still have time to prepare a simple meal.

Certainly, sir. Spicy cold noodles and lamb Szechuan, if that is all right with you.

It was. I made no recommendation concerning wine. I'd come to think he knew more about that than I.

Wolf thought my reflexes were slow and my timing was way off.

You don't have your usual level of concentration, he observed.

That was very true. However hard I tried to keep my mind on blocking Wolf's thrusts and finding an opening to attack him, my thoughts kept returning to my laptop. What new horror would I find when I fired it up? Having made an appointment to practice the next day, and every day thereafter except Sunday, which was Wolf's day off, I hurried home. Out of habit acquired fending off Abner Brown's thugs, I looked carefully for a tail. Nobody seemed to be following me, no one in sight whose presence on a quiet side street in my Upper East Side neighborhood seemed at all unusual. At home too everything was orderly and quiet. Feng met me at the door, offered me a glass of orange juice, and reported that his walk with Satan had produced the desired result.

His favorite spot on Madison Avenue, sir. He's a good dog, with good habits. Shall I bring your martini to the library now?

Thanks, Feng. I want one badly, but I'll take a bath and dress first.

Very little—perhaps nothing—in human behavior surprised or shocked Feng. He had seen too much. His father, a classical Chinese literature high-school teacher, being beaten to death by his students during the Cultural Revolution

before a crowd of spectators that included his mother, his
older sister, and himself, all three forced to watch, their arms
pinned back; his mother some days later throwing herself out
the fourth-story window of their apartment and surviving
as a quadriplegic whom his sister and he left behind in a Bei-
jing hospital when they were marched off into the countryside
for reeducation; his sister, who had been a good young violin-
ist, seeing her fingers become gnarled and covered with cal-
luses from work in the fields—these were his early memories.
His sister, by then married to a toothless peasant fifteen years
older than she, an outcome considered politically redeem-
ing for a girl of bourgeois background, was someone else
he left behind and never saw again after his own remarkable
skill as a wrestler came to the attention of the local party boss
and led to his being sent to the military academy in Shanghai. The other side of Feng was his rigor. Absolute rectitude,
unflinching courage, and, somewhat comically, a sense of
propriety in behavior and dress that I was sure would have
enchanted my Boston Brahmin grandmother. Therefore, his
asking whether I would like to have my martini in the library
while I was still in workout clothes meant simply that he
didn't forget that I was his employer and was free to do as I
pleased in my apartment. It didn't make it any less true that
I would have disappointed him if I had said yes: I might in
fact have hurt his feelings.

My respect for Feng's standards aside, the truth is that I
wanted my hot bath and wanted to change my clothes, and, in
early summer, if I was to keep Feng happy, that implied crisply
pressed chinos and a linen blazer. My shirt could be open

at the neck. Once the weather turned cool, he would have deplored anything less than a necktie or a turtleneck polo. I passed through my study on the way to my bath. There it was, on my desk, the violated, hacked laptop, my companion in the struggle to tame words and spin my stories, now inhabited by a malign force, the instrument of a deadly enemy. I resisted the temptation to open it. The Monster too could learn to wait. I'd get to him when I was ready.

There was, however, a limit to my self-discipline. I had vaguely thought of not looking at the computer until after dinner, but I couldn't hold out. Besides, I said to myself, by way of excuse, if I didn't look I'd be wondering what, if anything, was there and wouldn't be able to do justice to my martinis or Feng's lamb. Therefore, as soon as I had dressed, I went resolutely into my study, opened the laptop, and typed in my password. The cobra website came up:

You have a new notification

I clicked on those words and a message appeared:

For once you've found the mot juste, Dana. I am indeed a monster. Here is the link to my baby photo album. It will tell you more about suffering and hatred than you wish to know.

Once again, I followed the instructions. The images that appeared were not at all what I had expected—I'm not sure I knew or could describe what I expected. The first series consisted of headshots of an infant, not more than a month or two old, and perhaps younger. I suddenly realized that I had not known any newborn babies or even very young ones. The head was hideously misshaped. One ear was missing. One eye was way off to the side, covered by a flesh fold that was unlike an eyelid. The nose was off-center. I was accustomed to the appearance of malformed mouths from photographs, frequently appearing in ads seeking donations in the *Times,* of children with split lips and cleft palates. This mouth was similar, except that the images I'd seen before had all been of much older children. Somehow this being a baby's face made the deformation even more shocking. The headshots were followed by close-ups showing particular aspects of the face from different angles. The distance from the camera varied as well.

The age of the infant was revealed after I had scrolled down to the end of this series. A legend, the style and appearance of which made me believe I had been looking at a hospital record, read: Studies of Baby—the name was blacked out—at age of one month.

I took a deep breath, staggered rather than walked to the kitchen, got my martini from Feng, and made it back to my computer. Having downed a big slog, I scrolled to the next page and began to view the pictorial record of operations done on the child, with brief clinical descriptions and the child's age.

Ablation of the eye at the side of face and trimming of the flesh fold to prepare for subsequent installation of a

glass eye and creation of a simulacrum of an eyelid.
Age eighteen months.

A note specified that the eye that was removed was unseeing.

Repositioning and restructuring of the nose.
Age twenty-four months.

Breaking and restructuring of the jaw.
Age thirty months.

Pre-op and post-op photographs, taken from various angles, some zooming in on an aspect of the description, accompanied each procedure.

Many of these procedures were redone at twenty-four-month intervals. Photos succeeded photos.

On the last page, I came upon something called Medical History, Evaluation, and Comments. It appeared that this child was one of a pair of monoamniotic-monochorionic twins. I looked up these terms and found that the first meant that the twins shared the same amniotic sac in the mother's uterus and the second that they shared the same placenta. The pediatrician surmised that the pair had suffered from a condition relatively common in such very rare births, TTTS. That, I discovered, means twin-to-twin transfusion syndrome, which in turn means that because they share a placenta they also share blood supply, and the supply can become dangerously unbalanced, leading to deformations such as those exhibited by this particular child and potentially grave medical conditions in the twin who is on the short end of the supply. In the case of the child under study and treatment, those included impaired hearing, epilepsy, and uncontrolled tremor of the left arm and left leg, although it did not seem to include other symptoms that would be indicative of cerebral palsy. The hypothesis as to this child being the "donor twin," the twin giving its rightful share of the blood to the "recipient twin," and the adverse effect of receiving too much blood could not be studied because of the report received that the recipient twin had died. By reason of other particular circumstances of the case, it could not be ascertained whether the mother had suffered from chorioamnionitis. An infection, I also learned, of the uterus caused by bacteria traveling upward from the vagina, usually during prolonged labor.

I searched for a date or some indication of the hospital where all this had taken place. There was none.

There was a box at the end of the picture show with a caption: Comments. Without pausing to reflect, I typed:

> If this is really you as a baby I lack words to express my sympathy with your suffering, and that of your parents. Forgive me for calling you Monster. I was referring to what seem to be your moral qualities, not what may be your appearance.

I finished typing and clicked on a button labeled Send. At once I was returned to the previous page. A whirling circle

appeared, signaling new activity, and, in short, the following
appeared:

> I note that in addition to all your other defects, Dana,
> you're mawkishly sentimental. A quality deplorable in
> all circumstances, and in yours utterly laughable. Don't
> waste your pity on me: you will need every ounce of it
> for yourself and the Jewish slut.

Feverishly, I answered:

> Don't be so sure of that, Monster. And, by the
> way, where and why did you pick up such fluent
> Abnerspeak?

A new message appeared at once:

> Goodbye. You've been timed out.

I made it to the library—it seemed to me that I was a bit
unsteady on my feet—threw myself into an armchair, and
eagerly reached for the drink and the stuffed egg offered by
Feng, who appeared instantly, as though he'd been following
my movements on surveillance cameras. Yet to my knowledge, there were none in the apartment. Was it possible that
he had installed them on the sly? I scrutinized the tops of
the bookshelves and the ceiling. Nothing. The suspicion was
absurd.

. . .

Twin brother. Donor twin. Recipient twin. I turned these concepts over in my mind as I worked my way through the dinner Feng placed before me and somewhat more than half of the bottle of Beaune-Villages. It was more than I usually allowed myself, but he'd chosen the wine expertly. It was just right with the spicy lamb. He'd picked it out of the wine merchant's catalog and suggested that I buy at least three cases. It's a wine that can be drunk now, and it can also wait, he told me. The wines you inherited from your uncle, sir, will take us through the first few months of next year. Then all that will be left are the very exceptional bottles. I encouraged him to buy the Beaune, and whatever else he thought was appropriate. That was before the Monster made his appearance. Now I wondered whether I needed to worry about replenishing my cellar. Twin brother. Donor twin. Recipient twin. What appeared to be a vendetta pursued by a twin who talked like a clone of Abner—without Abner's obscenities. A twin—if the medical history the Monster posted wasn't simply a fake put together to confuse me—but whose twin? The recipient twin, according to the medical history, died. Abner was widely known to be an only child. But suppose that the recipient twin did not die? What if that part of the medical history was wrong, based on misinformation, or had been tampered with? Circumstances that prevented ascertaining whether the twins' mother had suffered from the disease—whatever its name—that traveled from the vagina to the uterus, and presumably had caused the sepsis in the recipient twin? What kind of circumstances were they? Might that also be misinformation, intentionally offered?

Unlike their son, Abner Brown's parents were not extraordinarily rich, but the research I'd done when I realized it was he who had commissioned the murder of my uncle Harry showed them to have been solidly well off, their wealth drawn principally from the state-chartered bank in Lubbock the father owned, and ranching. The bank, I supposed, had been sucked up into Abner's criminal enterprise and was a conduit for drug cartel money. But that came much later. It should be possible, I thought, to comb local birth records, as well as back issues of the local newspapers. It seemed likely that Abner's birth and any serious illness of Mrs. Brown *mère,* concerning, as they did, leading citizens, were likely to have been noted in the Lubbock newspaper. And it should be possible to go through the records of the hospital where she gave birth. A delivery of twins would not have taken place at home, even with a midwife and, perhaps, a doctor in attendance.

Logically, this was a job for the FBI. That meant I had to show Edwards the medical history, if it was still accessible on my computer. Instinctively, for reasons I couldn't immediately define, I preferred to keep this knowledge to myself. Nonsense, I knew perfectly well the reason: it was still my crazy idea that I would deal with the Monster all by myself, in my own way, without anyone's help, except perhaps Feng's. Crazy and absurd. I had no right to conceal this information from Edwards, and I had better get used to the fact that there would be no Wild West shoot-out between the Monster and me. I hadn't even managed to kill Abner. I had only been lucky enough to make suicide his only way out of the corner into which I'd driven him. You don't get lucky like that twice.

I asked Feng to hold off making my coffee until I'd returned from my study and rushed to see where matters stood on my computer. When I clicked on the file that had displayed the Monster's medical history, I received in its place a message:

The file you have requested is not available at this time.

That was that. I couldn't really blame myself for the file's having disappeared before I had shown it to Edwards. If there were a means of capturing it so that it remained on my laptop, I didn't know it. I would have to rely on my memory and relay to Edwards as accurately as possible what I had seen. The task should not be too difficult, I told myself. The images and words seemed burned in my memory, as though I had been branded.

I finished the coffee, and when Feng reappeared in the library and asked whether I would like another espresso or a whiskey, I told him that just before dinner I'd received new information from the Monster that I thought might be of the highest importance. Unfortunately, when I checked my laptop again moments ago, the file had disappeared. I would have to report on it in detail to Special Agent Edwards and also to Scott, and I would want him, Feng, to listen in. That was why I was not going to give him an account immediately. It was too late, in my opinion, to call either Edwards or Scott; I'd call them in the morning. Right now, I'd take Satan out for his good-night walk. And I'd certainly want a drink when I came back.

Sir, answered Feng, I know you will not be pleased to hear this, but I truly think you should leave the good-night walk to me. Or please allow me to accompany you. You are in real danger when you walk Satan alone after dark.

I understand, Feng, I said, and I don't mind your speaking up. Not in the least. But I want to take a walk with the dog. I need to clear my head, and that's the best way. Don't worry. I'll be very careful.

Very well, sir. I'll get Satan ready.

I went to my bathroom, urinated, and washed my hands. The face in the mirror looking back at me could have been that of a madman. Had I gone mad? Had I really seen the Monster's beginnings on my laptop screen? Had I put to him the question about Abnerspeak? I shook my head, splashed cold water on my face, and, after I'd dried it, dabbed it with shaving lotion.

Feng and Satan were waiting for me at the front door. He'd put Satan's yellow slicker on him and, in reply to my questioning look, told me a light drizzle was falling. I thanked him, put on the waterproof jacket he held for me, and rang for the elevator. Emil, the night man who'd been on duty the morning of my encounter in the park with the two thugs, was at the building's front door. Aha, the night shift had begun. He and Satan were buddies. I handed him the box with treats Feng had put in the pocket of my jacket and said, Emil, you'd better give one or two to your best friend. Mustn't disappoint him.

The caresses took some minutes. As soon as they were over, I whistled, Satan, come! We crossed Fifth Avenue and headed uptown. There were often runners on that side of the avenue, on their way to the Seventy-Ninth Street entrance or home, having finished their run. Perhaps because of the drizzle, I saw no one other than a dog walker coming toward me, a very large black Rottweiler on his leash, which he held short. As was his custom when another dog approached, Satan stopped and stood absolutely still, taking stock of the situation.

It's all right, Satan, I told him, that's a nice dog with a nice man, we'll ask whether you and his dog can say hello.

Good evening, I called out, is your dog friendly? Mine is super friendly. Would it be all right if they talked to each other?

He was a big man, not so tall as I but heavier, and dressed like all male Upper East Side dog walkers in a combination of army and hunting garments. He had an army fatigue cap on his head.

Very friendly, came the heavily accented answer. Another Hispanic or Brazilian, I said to myself. They really have a lock on that profession.

Satan wasn't buying this, not for the moment. He sank into his halt-who-goes-there crouch and waited. If he were another kind of dog, he would have been barking. But that is something French bulldogs don't do, except when someone they haven't yet recognized as a good person is at the door. Should you be foolish enough to try to take away what they consider their property—a toy or a bone or a piece of bagel that fell from the table and they've snatched—they will snarl a warning. You disregard it at your peril, because that is when these gentlest of dogs turn pitiless and ready to take your hand off.

The dog walker advanced. When the distance between us had shrunk to perhaps three yards he spat out a command I didn't catch and dropped the Rottweiler's leash. Instantly, the dog sprang forward, but not at me. He was going to attack Satan. Fortunately, the little Frenchie had gotten up from his crouch and I was able to scoop him under my left arm. As I did so, the Rottweiler leaped to follow Satan. I am six feet four; he couldn't reach my dog and sank his teeth instead into my forearm. The bite was powerful, but it could not penetrate the waxed sleeve of my waterproof Barbour jacket. He was suspended there, all hundred ten or hundred twenty pounds of him. My right hand was free. I reached into the pocket, found the switchblade, and did the only thing that I thought was possible: I cut the Rottweiler's throat; that would be sufficient, I hoped, and I would not be forced to disembowel him. It did suffice. The beautiful animal's jaw went slack, and he fell to the ground. Meanwhile, the dog walker had now drawn his own knife and was coming for me at a run. I wasn't ready for knife play, not with Satan cradled under my arm. I retreated a few paces, until my back was against the wall that separates Fifth Avenue from the park, and, when he lunged at me, I used a trick I'd learned at a martial arts studio in Venice and had been practicing with Wolf. Braced against the wall, I kicked the dog walker in the stomach as hard as I could. This was something he hadn't expected. The pain was surely almost unbearable. He doubled over. That is what I had been waiting for, the moment when he would involuntarily lower his head. I kicked again hard, my foot connecting with his mouth. I was wearing J.M. Weston loafers. The impact was enough to send the son of a bitch writhing to the ground, but I wished I'd worn combat boots instead. I set Satan on the ground, told him to sit, and looked the dog walker over. He was bleeding from his mouth. Probably, I knocked out a bunch of his teeth. Instinctively, I reached for my phone and was about to dial 911, when I thought better of it. This guy had been sent to have his dog maul and probably kill Satan. Was he going to tackle me next? Somehow, I didn't think that was part of the plan.

There were better uses for my time than waiting for the police cruiser, explaining what had happened, accompanying the walker to the police station, filling out forms. I took careful aim and kicked the prone figure in the head once again, hard, aiming this time for the temple. The Rottweiler's rattle had stopped. I was glad of that. I didn't have to give him the coup de grâce.

Let's go, Satan, I said. Make your mess as quickly as you can because we want to get home.

The rain had stopped. Either he understood me and decided to cooperate, or the emotions of the past ten minutes had had the effect one might think likely. The next big rooted tree appealed to Satan's sensibilities. Like the good citizen I am when it comes to ordinary duties, I scooped up, told Satan he was a very good boy, and crossed the avenue without waiting for the green light. Two blocks' quick walk south, and we were at my building. Emil was still on duty.

Nice walk, sir? Satan, were you a good dog?

Was it my imagination and morbid suspiciousness, or was there a faint look of surprise on Emil's face when he saw us return so calmly from our outing? Dog walkers seem glued to their cell phones. Had Satan's buddy Emil tipped this particular walker off to our arrival? Would he do such a thing to Satan? I hoped that if he did indeed finger us it was in the belief that I was the designated victim, and that Satan would not come to harm.

There was an undisguised look of worry on Feng's face as he took off Satan's raincoat and rubbed him dry with a towel. That task finished, he said, Excuse me, sir, but you and Satan must have had an unpleasant encounter. I saw the tear in the left sleeve of your Barbour jacket when I hung it in the coat closet as well as what seems to be a bloodstain, and when I checked whether the knife was in your pocket I saw traces of blood on the handle. May I ask you what happened?

Of course, I said. I wasn't going to conceal it from you. Anyway, it's something that I must tell Special Agent Edwards about right away, even though it's so late. Why don't you give Satan his snack and bring me a stiff bourbon to the library? I'll call Edwards from there and you can listen to the conversation.

VII

ir, you really just left them there, him and the dog?
I'd just finished describing Satan's and my encounter with the Rottweiler and his handler, and
Special Agent Edwards sounded a tad shocked. Feng, whom
I'd invited to listen in on our telephone call, was keeping a
straight face, but I thought I could detect something like an
approving twinkle in his eyes.

Yes, Joe, I did, but look at it this way: I'll give you odds,
ten to one, that this fellow knows my name and address. If
he wants to tell me off, all he has to do is cross the avenue—
assuming he can walk. If he wants to swear out a complaint,
that should have been a cinch too. The Nineteenth Precinct
station house is on East Sixty-Seventh Street. And if he isn't
up to walking, he can hail a cab. Or call 911 and get the cops
to drive him over.

I was trying hard not to laugh.

Considering that you wounded him, sir, you're taking this
very lightly.

This was a sententious side of Edwards. It surprised me.

If you don't mind, he continued, I'll hang up now, make a couple of calls to find out whether anything has been reported. Call you back in five.

Great idea, I replied, and asked Feng for another drink. I thought I deserved it.

More than ten minutes passed before the phone rang. Once again, I told Feng to listen in.

Nothing's been reported, sir, Edwards said. Your hunch was right. This guy is almost certainly a hit man and not a walker whose dog got out of control. It's a pity, though, if you don't mind my saying so, that you didn't call 911 and get him apprehended. We would at least know who he is and perhaps get him to talk.

Joe, I really doubt it. For instance, those guys with cudgels who attacked me in the park. Have the cops gotten anything from them?

No, sir.

The same way I don't think they would have gotten anywhere with this fellow. Incidentally, has the Westchester group made any progress?

None.

I thought so. I have a great deal more to tell you that relates specifically to the Monster. Can we get together tomorrow morning?

Certainly, sir. Would nine o'clock be too early?

I assured him it wouldn't.

I finished my drink and told Feng I was going out to check on whether the body of the dog was still there. What I didn't tell him was that the principal reason I wanted to know wasn't curiosity about how this fellow and his employers operated but, instead, a mixture of pity and regret. I've killed many men, but I had never before consciously killed an animal. Perhaps some animals died when my platoon and I fought our way through the streets of Fallujah, but that couldn't be helped. There was a convenient phrase for it: collateral damage. This was different. The Rottweiler had been a beautiful, courageous, and I'm sure very intelligent dog. It wasn't his fault that he had been trained to attack, and that his handler sicced him on Satan.

May I accompany you, sir? Feng asked.

Yes, I'd like you to, I told him. But let's leave Satan at home.

It had stopped raining. I led Feng to the exact spot. The dog's body had been removed. By whom? The walker? Street cleaners, who are so astonishingly active in this neighborhood? Feng said he could see traces of blood and pointed with his finger. Yes, there it was on the cobbles, between the sidewalk and the wall against which I had braced myself.

Nothing that had happened so far seemed to fall within the bailiwick of the Agency in McLean, but I knew that Scott Prentice would want to know about anything that put me in danger. I called him as soon as I woke the next morning and said I had asked Joe Edwards to come over to hear about new developments concerning the Monster. Would he like to participate via the phone loudspeaker? You bet I would, was the answer. That being settled, I told him briefly about the events of the past evening. His comment was: These people aren't just vicious. They're crazy, totally raving mad. First, the butchery on Penwood Road. Second, high-tech harassment and threats. Followed by two clownish, bungled aggressions. Can you think of anything equally absurd?

I can't, I answered, but I have this idea that you'll probably find equally absurd. What if we are dealing with acts of pure disinterested evil? Serving no purpose other than to hurt, to do harm?

I'll ponder that one. Offhand, it sounds crazy, just like those guys. Maybe that's why it's on target. Be sure you plug me in at nine, or whenever you start your meeting with Edwards. I'll be in the office, but you should call my cell-phone number.

I suggested to Edwards that we talk in the dining room, over Feng's freshly baked pound cake and coffee. Edwards had already tasted Feng's cuisine and readily agreed. With his permission, I called Scott and put him on the loudspeaker. Feng remained in the room, and I succeeded in prevailing on him to sit down, eat some of his own cake, and drink some of his fragrant boiling-hot coffee. This would be the first time for him as well to hear about the Monster's ghastly medical history.

I can't stop blaming myself, I said, for not having found some way to preserve those photos, the text, and the exchange of messages. Perhaps there was some way to do it. But I was too shaken by what I saw to try to figure it out.

There was, Edwards told me gently. You could have taken screen shots, or photos of the laptop screen. With your cell-phone camera.

I'm sorry to say that I don't even know what a screen shot is, and the thought of using my camera never occurred to me. Fortunately, my recollection of what I saw is clear, and I think I'll be able to describe it accurately.

That turned out to be a fair assessment, and it left Edwards and Scott momentarily speechless. The silence was broken by Feng.

Sir, he said, the condition described in what appeared on your laptop is probably rare. The operations to correct the defects are perhaps even rarer. Would it be possible to search medical journals for references to such a case? They might lead one to the hospital where they were performed, or something similar.

Very good thinking, Feng, said Edwards. I don't know whether archives of leading medical journals have been digitized, or how far back digitization goes, but there must be indexes and other ways to zero in on this subject. Really good thinking! We'll get some analysts on it.

Yes, indeed, Scott chimed in, that should be in addition— same level of priority, I would think—to following up your idea that the Monster's dominant twin in fact survived and was none other than Abner Brown. Lubbock wasn't exactly a metropolis when Abner was born. Would that have been in '30? '31?

Much later, I think, I answered, more like 1941 or '42. He was a relatively young man.

Doesn't matter. Unless the mother went to Houston or Dallas for the delivery, looking for a bigger and better hospital, it should be fairly easy to track this down in Lubbock.

One could also take, let's say, 1940 as the start of the search of medical literature. And if that's a dry hole, one might try Houston and Dallas. Are we loading you up with too much, Joe?

No, sir, Joe answered, that's the sort of thing the Bureau does well, and I'll make sure we get on it.

All right, Scott continued, let me ask you a more difficult question. The event of yesterday evening. Did I misunderstand what Jack told me? I think he said he'd be under FBI protection. Discreet, probably invisible, but definitely there. What went wrong yesterday? And may I ask whether, as a general matter, you feel, as I do, that the investigation is somehow or other in low gear? What's going on?

Edwards actually turned red. He held out his cup for Feng to refill it, drained it, and in the end said: May I speak absolutely off the record? Will everybody here keep what I tell him to himself?

Of course, said Scott. Feng and I nodded.

All right. What happened yesterday, I mean the lack of protection, sounds to me like an ordinary fuckup. Please excuse my language. Probably our guy thought the captain had called it a day. There is something else, though. I think you know, certainly you know it, Mr. Prentice, that law-enforcement agencies, and particularly the Bureau, are under unusual pressures. Everybody knows about the director. That has sunk in and then some. Many of us think that's terrible and are determined to push back. There are others, and it's hard to be sure who stands where in this, who are in sync with some of this stuff. These pressures don't involve only the investigation that's constantly in the news. They go in many directions. Unpredictable. One doesn't always know why. But they are being exerted. And they may be effective. As I said, it's not just the Bureau. It could be the state police. It could be the local cops. I can't tell. But I can promise you that I'm doing my job without regard to any of this shit, and that I will break my ass to make sure the research gets done. And, of course, that the captain doesn't get killed and this case is solved. Oh, and by the way, Feng. My contact at the NYPD has told me your concealed carry permit will be available tomorrow. You should pick it up ASAP.

Scott said he had to hang up to go to a meeting with his boss, a real politician, he observed. I'll call you later, he added.

I felt exhausted by the effort to tell my story accurately and the implications that were emerging ever more starkly. It was eleven-thirty. One could say with some assurance that the sun was over the yardarm.

Shall we have a drink? I asked Edwards. Feng mixes a mean Bloody Mary. If you wish, he can go light on the vodka.

I'd like that a lot, was the answer, very light on the vodka, please. I have to report on this stuff and need to figure out how to control the flow of information.

Feng came back with the drinks. As I expected, he refused my invitation to have one himself and reminded me it was time for Satan's walk. He would serve lunch as soon as he and the Frenchie got back.

No, thanks, Feng, I said. I'll take him out this time. Once more, I need to clear my head, and before he could begin to protest I added that I fully understood the risk but very much wanted to see what, if anything, would happen. And, just in case, I'd slip the Colt in the pocket of my jacket, as well as the switchblade.

Do you think I'm crazy, Joe? I asked.

Just one moment, he replied. I'll make a quick call. He stepped out of the dining room. When he returned it was to say, Go right ahead, sir. Take the hardware, by all means, but you're covered. No fuckup today, not yet.

It was late evening when Scott and I finally spoke.

That Edwards is a good guy, he said, as good as advertised. But what a shitty moment in our history! It makes one long for J. Edgar Hoover and Richard M. Nixon.

A strange calm followed those agitated days. I spoke with Heidi every morning her time, after her breakfast, which came out to be right after my dinner. The arbitration in Hong Kong was still on the right track. The flight to Tokyo had been uneventful; her clients had sent a car to pick her up at Haneda Airport and take her to the hotel. She was at the Four Seasons, where she had never stayed before, but she found it so pleasant that she didn't mind not staying at the Okura, her home away from home in Tokyo until it closed. The meetings with her clients were also going well. In fact, she thought she might be able to return to New York a couple of days earlier than previously planned.

Now, now, Captain. She laughed when I told her excitedly that in that case we should go to Sag Harbor as soon as she arrived, to take advantage of the beautiful weather predicted for the next ten days. I'd pick her up at Kennedy, and we'd drive directly to Long Island instead of Fifth Avenue.

Now, now, Captain, you forget that I'm a working girl and a valued member of my firm's litigation team. I must go to the office directly from the plane and take care of some stuff my secretary has told me about. But I'll clear the decks for a short vacation just as fast as I can. Cheer up! I won't be working nights, and there are two pairs of silk pajamas, one white and one red, I had made for me in HK! I think you might like helping me get out of them!

She said nothing about Feng's friends who had stood guard over her in Hong Kong, or the Krohn security operatives who, according to her father, would have arranged to shadow her in Tokyo. They all must have been very discreet. It was hardly the sort of thing she wouldn't mention if she'd suspected anything, and it was quite a trick not to arouse her curiosity. She was a very observant and inquisitive young lady.

The search of medical literature produced one hit, an article in a 1945 issue of the *New England Journal of Medicine* describing the case of twins that corresponded so precisely to what the Monster had let me see that I would have thought he had simply uploaded pages from the journal if the material that appeared on my laptop screen had not been even more extensive. Unfortunately, the journal didn't mention the hospital at which the delivery or the procedures had taken place, or the relevant dates—let alone the names of the twins or their parents. Its files indicated that the author, a Dallas pediatric surgeon who died in the 1960s, had specified that the parents consented to the publication on condition that this information never be disclosed.

This doesn't prove that your Monster is Abner's twin, said Edwards, but the date of publication, if you put it together with the fact that the last photo was of a thirty-month-old child, does not make birth in 1940 or '41 impossible, and the fact that the author was Dallas-based is another indication backing up your theory.

Scott, who was listening to our conversation, agreed.

All right, I said, but where does that take us?

That's a good question, sir. I'm not sure, but one area of research would be to look for a possible financial or control connection between Brown Enterprises or his foundation or anyone or anything that might correspond to your Monster.

That's something we might conceivably help with, mused Scott. We have an old, and I hope still abiding, interest in the extracurricular activities of Brown Enterprises. Send me a pdf of that article, Joe, would you?

Yes, sir. As soon as we finish here.

I'll tell you what I think. I decided to weigh in, at the risk of sounding like a stuck record. You'll be looking for a needle in a haystack, a needle that, by the way, may not exist. What basis do we have for thinking that there is a financial or control relationship between this son of a bitch and the Brown businesses? He never surfaced in any way while Abner was alive. Just as probably, he's running his own business, if you want to call it that, and he killed the Lathrops and he's after me in some even more bizarre and sinister way because, for reasons we don't know, but I'd sure like to know, he's out to avenge Abner. Why? Brotherly love? Why would he love the twin who sucked life out of him? You tell me. I know you can't. But there may well be another motive or perhaps a mixture of motives. He might show his hand enough for us to understand it. Whatever it is, I somehow think we will nail the Monster only if I goad him into coming after me directly, so that we finally lock horns.

Lock horns with him, brother? said Scott. It will just get you killed.

Amen, chimed in Edwards.

Depressed or fired up by this exchange—I wasn't sure I could tell which feeling predominated—I went over the notes about Abner's start in life I'd made shortly after my uncle Harry was murdered. Born January 12, 1941, in Lubbock, Texas. Father commissioned in the U.S. Navy shortly after Pearl Harbor. A desk assignment in D.C., dealing with procurement. Upon return to Texas, added to a ship-supply business in the Port of Texas City. Possibly drawing on connections made while in service. Business miraculously escaped destruction in the 1947 explosions and fires, expanding rapidly instead in Texas City and the Port of Houston. Family moved to Houston in the early fifties, and the center of gravity of his businesses moved there as well. Father died at the beginning of the 1960s, and Abner, recently graduated from Princeton and ostensibly the only child, took over the reins of the business. Early 1970s: mother murdered. Unsolved crime, committed in her mansion at the Royal Oaks Country Club. All this I vaguely knew, since it was the prelude to the accumulation of Abner's colossal fortune that raised him to the very first rank of American billionaires, and his perversion of the family business into an international crime empire. But where in that story was there room for a twin like the Monster? Perhaps there was not any because no such twin existed. Perhaps there was no consanguinity between the Monster and Abner, and the Monster's diction and murderous viciousness were a case of unexplained mimesis.

Checking my hacked laptop was a rite I found myself performing several times a day. The cobra icon was still there. It opened readily. Nothing new had been posted. I fiddled around idly, found the Comments button, and clicked on it. A dialogue box appeared. I moved my cursor to it and started typing.

> Hello, Monster, was Abner Brown your "recipient twin," the twin who drained, because you shared your mother's placenta, the blood and nutrition that you should have received?

I clicked on the Send button.

There followed some activity on the site that made me think it was writhing. After it had quieted down, a message appeared:

> Inquiries deemed appropriate are answered in the order received.

All right. I wasn't in a hurry, so long as I could catch up on the fake news peddled by the failing *NYT* while I waited. The link was bookmarked. That site too opened with alacrity. The president, I learned, had told Russian officials at a meeting in the White House that firing James Comey had relieved him of great pressure he'd been under because of the investigation into possible collusion between his campaign and the Russians. That's nice, I said to myself. I'm sure the boys and girls at the FBI will be glad to hear about it. Cheered by that thought, I decided to check on the Monster.

There was an answer to my inquiry. Composed in fluent Abnerspeak, it read as follows:

Suck it up, fuckhead! Le pire est toujours certain. Knowing the answer to your question—which, by the way, is none of your business—wouldn't save you or the Jewish slut.

A reply was in order. I gave in to my worst instincts and typed:

You're a real asshole, Monster. Your brain got fucked, as well as your face and whatever else there you've got by way of a body. Otherwise, would you be avenging the twin whose existence caused you all that misery? The twin who turned you into a piece of shit? You should be glad he's dead. You should be fucking grateful to me. I put to you these questions because if there is any part of your brain that's capable of introspection I would like to help you.

If the goal was to be obscene and offensive, I thought my message probably made the cut. If I wanted to open a dialogue, it was idiotic. Our correspondence was displayed in full. A photo seemed in order. I snapped one, closed my laptop, and obeyed Feng's summons to lunch.

Over spicy prawns followed by an eggplant casserole, I reflected on what should be my next move. That the novel was going badly was hardly news. Who could expect it to go well with the Monster in the background? I asked myself. The only solution was to work on it. Keep typing. Advance as much as you can and rewrite to get the text into the best shape possible. With luck, get new ideas that will give this mishmash a lift. Easier said than done, of course, but, as I kept reminding myself, these woes were self-inflicted. Nobody obliged me to be a novelist. I had enough money to live on. If writing was too hard, who said I couldn't simply quit? Yes, but if I quit, who would I be? An early bloomer and fader, dogged by violence and bloodshed. Would Heidi want to go on living with me and continue the tenuous, delicate process of accepting sex with such a man? How large a part did my success as a writer play in my appeal? The thought of losing Heidi—or of her losing interest in me—was intolerable. Besides, writing raised me out of an abyss of harrowing memories and dark thoughts to a different, sometimes higher plane, into a world of my creation. Or so I hoped.

The calendar was another subject for reflection. Memorial Day was approaching. Heidi should certainly be back before then, and I couldn't believe that my beloved, hardworking, crack litigating partner would claim she was too busy to come with me for three days to Sag Harbor. Especially since on one of those days she could visit her parents in East Hampton. I wouldn't take no for an answer. That meant, however, that I should definitely go to Sag Harbor tomorrow, just to avoid surprises when I arrived there with Heidi. For various reasons, most of them related to Heidi's workload, I hadn't been to my house since Easter, that is to say since mid-April. Of course, deep down inside I knew there wouldn't be any surprises. Mary Murphy, the wonderful young housekeeper who had worked for my uncle Harry and had stayed on with me, made sure the house was always in perfect order. Had anything gone wrong, she would have gotten in touch immediately. She loved to communicate almost as much as she loved to take care of the house. No, the stuff about avoiding surprises was an excuse: the real reason for going to Sag Harbor on a Saturday morning was that I wanted to. I missed the house, the garden, and the beach on which, in the off-season, Satan and I could walk at any hour of the day. And, to tell the truth, I missed Mary and my next-door neighbor, the painter Sasha Evans. Now that Simon Lathrop had been murdered, they were my sole remaining links to Harry.

Feng, I said, I've decided to go to Sag Harbor tomorrow and to talk Miss Heidi into joining me there for the Memorial Day weekend. I could leave this afternoon, but the traffic is going to be bad. I'd rather go tomorrow.

He had cleared the table and was busy serving dessert. Orange slices doused with gin. The gin seasoning was his invention, one of which I was deeply appreciative. He looked at me quizzically. I thought I knew what he was going to say. To save him the trouble, I told him, Yes, Feng, I know I shouldn't go alone. So if you don't mind missing your Sunday afternoon, please come to Sag with Satan and me. And take off any weekday afternoon you like next week.

VIII

had loved the vacations I was allowed to spend alone
with my uncle Harry in Sag Harbor once it was
decided I was old and reliable enough to travel from
Boston to New York City or Sag Harbor, I loved learning to
sail his daysailer sloop, and I loved being taught by him, with
infinite patience, how to handle myself in the Atlantic surf.
Harry had never married, he had no children. It was natu-
ral that he should leave to me the Sag Harbor house and the
apartment on Fifth Avenue in which I live. The house itself,
an early nineteenth-century structure that had miraculously
escaped the fire of 1845 that destroyed much of Sag Harbor,
was a warren of small rooms, many of them strangely shaped.
It did, however, boast a fine upstairs master bedroom that
I now called Heidi's room and, across the corridor, a nice
principal guest room that had become officially my room. As
a practical matter that meant that I kept my clothes there.
Never since the first Christmas that we spent in the house
together, soon after Abner Brown's suicide, had Heidi barred

the door against me. It was, she told me then, because she wanted to cuddle. The cuddling had progressed and turned into lovemaking as ardent as any I had ever known, and happier, because it turned out that I had come to love Heidi more than I had loved anyone before. The garden was small, as in all those old houses, but beautifully designed and tended. Harry had refused to give up any part of it for the sake of installing a swimming pool, and I agreed one hundred percent. With the ocean beaches—Gibson Lane, in Sagaponack, was our favorite—at most twenty minutes away, and the Sound beaches, to which we rarely went, even nearer, I didn't think I needed a pool. The house was complemented by a high-ceilinged, insulated, and heated studio, with its own bath, that had originally been a barn. Harry had used it as his office, and that is where Abner Brown's hit man Slobo murdered him. That is also where, some months later, I mortally wounded Slobo. Notwithstanding this history, I made Harry's studio my office, where I liked best to work on my books.

Mary Murphy was incorrigible. Although I had told her there was no need to be at the house on a Saturday morning, there she was, greeting Feng and me with infectious enthusiasm. Satan was the special object of her affection. She picked him up, called him her love, gave him two huge treats from a plastic envelope she kept in her pocket, and let him out into the garden.

How many weeks has it been, Jack? she asked.

I had prevailed upon her to call me by my first name, rather than Captain.

Too many, I answered, and all for stupid reasons. Such as

Heidi's having too much work to come out. Or me trying to finish something I was trying to write. Or having to do a reading. I'm putting an end to all that. I hope to be out every weekend from now on, and to stay in Sag Harbor from mid-June until the end of September.

That is the best news, Jack! she cried. Will you and Feng have a drink, or would you like some tea?

I'm going to surprise you, Mary, I answered. I'd really like a big cup of tea. And you, Feng?

The same, Miss Mary.

Let's have it right here, in the kitchen, I told her.

I was sipping the scalding hot tea and listening to Mary's account of her and her husband's pet shop in Wainscott, on Route 27, when the landline telephone rang.

Surprised, and somewhat worried, unexpected and untimely calls having too often in the past turned out to be from Abner Brown's thugs and were now in my mind associated with the Monster, I looked at the caller-ID window: PRIVATE CALLER. I picked up, overcoming my initial instinct to let whoever it was leave a message if he was so inclined.

Jack, said a voice I recognized but didn't place immediately, Jack, this is Jon, Jonathan Krohn.

Heidi's father.

Yes, Jon, hello! How amazing that you found me here.

Not really, Jack, the message on your city voice mail said that if you weren't in the city you'd be in Sag Harbor, at this number. I was only following instructions. Jack, we're in East Hampton. I need to see you. Urgently.

Of course, I answered. I've just gotten here. Shall I drive over to your place right now or after lunch?

After lunch will be fine, he answered, and I'd rather see you at your house. We need to speak privately. Two-thirty? Three?

Whichever you prefer.

The fashion magnate liked to split the difference. At quarter of three, then, he told me.

It was a few minutes past one. Mary was getting ready to leave. I told her she really didn't need to come to the house tomorrow—Feng would look after me—and that I expected Heidi and I and probably Feng would be out next Friday evening, for the long weekend. Or perhaps sooner, if Heidi got back from Japan sooner.

That will be really nice, she exclaimed and threw her arms around me.

And Feng, I said, don't start making lunch, we're going to have a quick bite at the American Hotel. But perhaps you'd like to take Satan out for a little walk first and make sure he does his business.

Satan is the first French bulldog I've known, and I don't know whether fastidiousness is a characteristic of the breed or yet another aspect of Satan's remarkable tact. This dog, who never steals food and will not push open a door that has been left ajar, preferring to wait until he's been invited to come in or go out, has never wanted to poop in the garden. Peeing is all right, but, in order to defecate, Satan has to be off his own property.

I took my bag upstairs and unpacked, wondering what

could be behind Jon's urgent desire to see me. Something concerning Heidi? Logically, it should be that, but I had spoken with Heidi in the morning, before Feng and I left for the country and before she went to bed for the night, and everything in Tokyo seemed to be on an even keel. It would be Sunday in Japan when she woke up; there were no meetings scheduled. Just a lunch with the client's president and his wife at their favorite shabu-shabu restaurant, and a solo visit she planned to make to the National Museum followed by a walk in Ueno Park. I had smiled, thinking that she wouldn't be entirely on her own. If Krohn security was on the job, as I certainly hoped, she'd be trailed by a couple of operatives from the moment she left her hotel room until she had retired safely for the night. But if it wasn't Heidi, what could he want to see me about? No use speculating, I told myself. I'd find out soon enough.

I heard Satan's paws on the painted wooden floor in the entry, and a moment later Feng's report: He's done everything he needed to do, sir.

Let's go, then.

Feng set the alarm and locked the front door, a precaution I wouldn't have taken. But I wasn't going to argue. We were under siege.

The American Hotel had been Uncle Harry's favorite Sag Harbor hangout, I explained to Feng, whom I'd never taken there before, and it had become mine as well. We didn't have much time, so I ordered a club sandwich for myself, crab cakes for Feng—to my great relief he liked them—and two Montauk ales. We were back at the house at two-thirty. I checked the voice mail. Nothing.

I'll ask Mr. Krohn to meet with me in the studio, I told Feng. Please bring us coffee there. Or tea if he prefers it.

It was a mild afternoon. Satan stretched out in the sun on the flagstone patio outside the studio door. I was going to turn on the classical music station but thought better of it. We'd wait in silence. How many more blissfully quiet moments such as this one would be given to us to savor?

Jon Krohn arrived at precisely two forty-five.

No coffee, no tea, he said, I'm way too nervous. Just a glass of water, please, and I'll get on with my story.

He told it in bursts, interrupted by pauses during which this handsome athletic billionaire, so well barbered and so elegant in his blue linen suit and yellow silk shirt open at the collar, would sob and struggle to get himself under control. I had a fresh handkerchief in my jeans pocket and held it out. He took it, and nodded thanks.

His story boiled down to this. Heidi's brother, Mike, a couple of years her senior, his third wife, Lilly, and their little son, Jonjon, all of whom he'd mentioned during my recent visit to his office, as well as Jonjon's nanny, were unexpectedly staying with him and Helen in East Hampton. A visit that wasn't on the program. Mike called to say that they were coming three days ago and told his mother that there was a local holiday that made it convenient to take Jonjon out of kindergarten for a week or ten days to see the grandparents he is always asking about, and that anyway Lilly would like to have Jonjon see an American allergist. She thinks he may be allergic to shellfish. The following morning, they showed up. You should understand, Jon continued, that Mike is the nonexecutive chairman of Krohn Enterprises Asia, and he and his family live in Hong Kong, in a mansion off Mount Kellett Road, a short distance west from the Peak. Quite a piece of real estate, he added with a tinge of bitterness.

This information surprised me. Why hadn't Heidi told me that her brother and his family lived in Hong Kong? Had she not gone to see them? As an only child, I have a tendency to assume that brothers and sisters are always on the best of terms with each other. This could be a case of siblings who didn't get along.

We were surprised but naturally happy to see them, Jon continued. No, that's an understatement. Helen was ecstatic. Then first thing this morning, Mike asked to see me alone and said he's in very big trouble. He has just received yet another threatening call from a group trying to collect money on behalf of a Macao casino, where he lost big at blackjack. What do you mean big, I asked, and why haven't you paid? About two and a half million dollars U.S., Mike told me, and (a) I don't have the money, and (b) the dealer was cheating. He was using a fucking rigged shoe! I know you don't understand it, Dad, but trust me. I've been around, and I can tell. The SOB was cheating! So why did you go on, I asked, why didn't you go to the management or the police or wherever you go in such a case? I did stop, Mike replied. I got up and told the bastard I wanted to inspect the shoe. The other players all got up too, a bunch of Chinks. They were really riled up. The SOB told me to shove it, and I guess pressed some button to call the private casino cops. They grabbed me and hustled me to the manager's office. You don't argue with guys like that or try to fight your way out. I'd established credit at that shit-hole casino, so they knew I was basically good for the money and didn't even listen when I complained. The head Chink just said, Mr. Krohn, you settle up within forty-eight hours. That's the house rule. I hightailed it out of there, Dad, and out of Macao, and got Lilly, Jonjon, myself, and the nanny on the first flight out of Hong Kong I could book, and we came here. Where else was I supposed to run? I'm scared, Dad, I'm scared. When they called me on my cell phone today, they said they knew where I was. Your father's house in East Hampton! Somehow, they figured it out. We didn't tell anyone where we were going. Not Jonjon's nanny, we just put her on the plane, not the housekeeper, no one at the office. Literally, no one. We said we'd be back soon, that's all. And now the guy who called said if I don't pay what I owe plus the fine and expenses they'll take Jonjon. Jesus, Dad! What are we going to do?

How much will that be? I asked Mike, Jon continued. They said five million today, and it will be six million tomorrow and growing, so you better pay up, he told me. And I don't even know how to pay! The guy who called—you should have heard him, a fucking Chink asshole with a thick accent—didn't say. He said, Just get the money ready. In Bitcoin.

After Mike told me this story, my first move was to call my head of security and tell him we had better put his men on alert. So that's done. We've got a bunch of guys on duty. But that can't go on. Can't keep Mike and his family under lock and key forever, much as I'd like to. So I've come to you for help! For advice!

Do you know what casino Mike was at?

Yes, Star Casino.

And did the guy who called him say he works for Star?

No, he said specifically that the case was referred to them for collection. Don't bother with the casino. We're Yellow Flower.

You think I know about this sort of thing, Jon, I said, but the fact is I don't. All I know is that Mike seems to be in big trouble. Let me talk to my friend Feng.

Yes, your Chinese houseman. Heidi has told me about him.

That's right. But before he came to the States he was a member of a crack Hong Kong police unit. He knows all about the Hong Kong scene and, I imagine, Macao, and I know he still has a lot of friends on the force in Hong Kong. If you like, I'll talk to him right now, and see if he has any ideas.

Feng must have shopped for our dinner. I found him in the kitchen, busy chopping vegetables.

Lemon chicken, sir, and a spicy mixed-vegetables casserole, he told me. If you will allow me, sir, I'll take Satan out for a little walk as soon as I finish this. I need only ten minutes.

He waved his hand over the chopping board.

I thought we'd all three go for a walk on the beach, I replied, but first I must finish with Mr. Krohn. He has told me a terrifying story, and if you can stop your work for a moment I'll tell you what it's about. We need your advice.

Feng listened carefully, occasionally cracking his knuckles, a sign, I had learned, of considerable distress.

This is very bad, he said, finally. Star Casino. Bad reputation even when I was on the force. Yellow Flower. A new triad. After the war. Moved to HK from Shanghai. It was small then. I don't know the size now. Really bad people. No honor.

It sounded bad, I replied. Will you come and talk to Mr. Krohn? He's a good man.

It didn't take long for Feng to repeat, with some needed elaboration, what he had told me.

What should I do, then, Mr. Feng, Jon asked, what is your advice?

These are very dangerous people, sir. I understand you have security people working for you. Perhaps you need to bring in more security. They should watch not only Mr. Michael Krohn and his wife and little boy, but also you and Mrs. Krohn and Miss Heidi.

Understood, said Krohn. And the police?

Did the people Mr. Michael spoke to say anything about the police?

I don't think so, replied Jon. He didn't mention it.

Usually kidnappers and enforcers like Yellow Flower say, Don't go to the police. Perhaps the person who spoke to Mr. Michael isn't experienced and was picked to speak to him because he speaks English. There is a risk in going to the police, but this isn't a kidnapping case. They haven't got a kidnapped person they can hurt if you disobey.

Not yet, was the thought that went through my head.

So I think that probably it will be good to tell the police. Probably the FBI.

Jim Comey, the director who is my friend, has been fired,
mused Jon. So too bad. I still haven't gotten through to the
deputy. But I know one or two people who should be close to
him. I'll try to get put through. Tell me, Mr. Feng, should we
pay these people?

Mr. Krohn, excuse me, please, I have been away from
Hong Kong many years now and I have no current information. With your permission, I will call friends this evening
and get advice. What I say now is stale knowledge. We used
to think Yellow Flower aren't reliable people. If you pay an
old, established triad you can be sure: you pay up; they leave
you alone. With Yellow Flower, as it used to be, you can't be
sure. There is risk. But it is safer to pay. If Mr. Michael Krohn
decides to pay, he should get very complete instructions from
the people who call him, and say, I will pay and I will let the
casino know I am paying. But with your permission, sir, I can
give better information late this evening or tomorrow.

Please do call your friends and thank you for telling me all
this.

Jon, Feng, I interjected suddenly. A question: How does a
triad like that, one that isn't all that established, operate in
the U.S.? How do the triad members come into the country?
I don't understand.

You're right, sir, Feng answered. They can't do anything
here unless they have members already living in this country. An old triad has members here. Yellow Flower—unlikely.
They would partner with a gang, kidnappers, or killers that
operate in this country.

I see, I said. Since this affects Heidi's family, and she is also under threat, I think I must tell Joe Edwards about it. Joe, I added, is the FBI special agent I've been talking to. I think I've mentioned him to you, Jon.

Yes, I remember, the one I was going to mention to the deputy director, Jon said. And I think you're right. And, Mr. Feng, he continued, I'm most grateful to you. If your friends agree with your advice, we will follow it. We will step up security, we will call the police, and we will pay. Let's talk as soon as you're ready. Mrs. Krohn and I will be at home this evening, and you and Mr. Dana shouldn't hesitate to call me late. As late as eleven-thirty or midnight is all right. I'm sure I'll want to keep consulting with you and Mr. Dana, but I have to tell you that I already feel a little better, a little calmer. And now I should go home, before Helen starts to wonder what I'm doing. She realizes that something is wrong, but neither Michael nor I have told her that Jonjon is in danger.

As he got up to leave, my burner cell phone rang. The only people who called me on it were Heidi (but at this hour it was nighttime in Tokyo, and she should be asleep), Scott, and Joe Edwards.

Excuse me, Jon, I said. I had better answer.

It was Joe.

Captain Dana, sir, he said, I want to give some annoying news. Instructions have come down from management to lift the protection we've been providing you. The basis is that there hasn't been any overt incident or threat. I thought you ought to know this. I'm truly sorry.

Thanks for telling me, I replied, but please don't worry about it. Feng and I will manage just fine. I'm curious though: So far as your management was concerned, the thugs with cudgels in the park don't count? Or the incident with the attack Rottweiler doesn't count?

That's right. With respect to the incident in the park, they call it an attempted mugging. As for the stuff with the Rottweiler, they say that since you didn't call the police it was most likely just a dogfight.

I see. Have you got a few minutes? I was about to call you when you rang. There is something new that I think you should know about. Is this a good time to talk?

Jon Krohn nodded energetically, encouraging me.

Since Joe said he had all the time I needed, I related as succinctly as possible, without sacrificing significant details, Jon Krohn's story and Feng's take on it.

This is very bad, said Joe. Really bad. Did you say that Mr. Krohn will report all of this to the Bureau?

Jon jumped in.

Yes, Mr. Edwards, this is Jonathan Krohn speaking. Yes, I will report this to the Bureau, I hope through the deputy director's office, and, depending on what my Bureau contact tells me, to the local police and the NYPD as well.

That's great, sir, replied Joe. May I make a couple of interim suggestions?

Please do.

First, your son should record any call he gets from the extortionists. He has an iPhone?

Jon nodded energetically. Yes, he does.

Well, Apple doesn't make it easy to record a conversation, but it can be done, essentially by the Add Call function. A tricky maneuver, but if your son is telephone savvy he'll figure it out. He puts the caller on hold and plugs in his own cell phone—in effect calls himself—or calls one of your landlines that you dedicate to the purpose and that has a calls-will-be-answered function. If he has a problem, he should go to an Apple Store, and the people there will teach him.

There's one in Sag, I interjected. Michael can go over there and get it done. It's clearly very important.

Understood, Jon replied. Michael loves playing with his iPhone. I bet he can do it.

Good, Joe continued. You can see why that's very important. And you, sir, should get a burner, a phone with a prepaid card, and use it for your telephone conversations with Captain Dana and anyone else involved in helping you with this problem.

We'll get all that done, answered Jon. I'm most grateful for the advice. And now I've really got to run.

All right, Joe, thanks for everything, I said, trying to keep any hint of irony out of my voice. I'm going to accompany Mr. Krohn to the door.

May I stay on the line and have another word with you? Joe asked.

Certainly, I said.

On the way out, I gave Jon my burner number on a Post-it. Please use it for all calls, I told him.

As soon as I got back to the studio I picked up the phone and said, Joe, I'm here again, and I want to tell you that I'm really grateful for your being so helpful with Jon Krohn.

No problem, he answered. I just wanted to say this, sir, that it doesn't matter what the management said about lifting your cover. I'm staying with you, just as before. Twenty-four seven. I also want to tell you, and this is as confidential as anything can be, that they don't like you in some parts of our management. The idea is you have a big mouth and have been saying stuff about the president no American should say, and that you hounded a great American, Abner Brown, to his death. I think you understand what I mean.

Is this stuff coming from Texas, by any chance? I asked.

Joe chuckled. How did you guess?

Any specific ideas as to the source?

Suddenly, his voice became very serious. I don't know the source, sir. I sure wish I did.

What a mess, I said to Feng. I think that Satan understands that we've got problems. Did you notice how quiet he has been?

He's a very intelligent dog, sir, he replied, with strong feelings.

You're right. I think he really needs a walk now. A good walk on the beach and a chance to run with other dogs.

Yes, sir. May I come with you? I'll need to change shoes.

Do come, I told him. I have the feeling that something bad is brewing, and I agree with you and Joe, and Scott Prentice, that we should be very careful. What I'd call stupidly careful.

Both my uncle Harry and I were used to leaving the front door to the Sag Harbor house on the latch. At most, we locked it at night. It gave me a turn to see Feng once again set the alarm as we were leaving and lock the door.

This is crazy, I said. Nobody in this town lives like this. Perhaps an old maid or two. The windows are open. It's easy enough to cut the mosquito netting and climb in.

That's true, sir, but I've set the motion detector. Once whoever has climbed in starts moving around, the alarm will go off.

And what about going in through the garden gate and hunkering down in the studio? The door to the studio is wide open.

Sir, the garden gates are wired too. Someone can always find a way to get in, but the alarm makes it much harder.

Have it your way.

I opened the Volvo's tailgate and told Satan, We're going to the beach. Jump in!

"Beach" is a concept Satan understands and likes. He took off like a rocket, landed, and turned expectantly toward me.

Yes, Satan, here is a treat. You're a good dog.

Saturday the week before Memorial Day. As you would expect, the traffic was light everywhere, even on Route 27 when we crossed it. The vegetable stand on Sagg Main had not yet opened for the season. I pointed it out to Feng and said that when it opened that was where we'd get our lettuce, vegetables, and corn, usually on our way back from the beach.

Three or four cars were parked at the entrance to Gibson Lane beach.

You're going to like this beach, Feng, I told him, it's the most beautiful beach in the world. Totally unspoiled. No commercial establishments, no high-rises, just rich men's houses, and not too many of those. Anyway, most of the time there is no one living in them.

I had suddenly realized that although Feng had been to Sag Harbor before, with Heidi and me, it was in the winter, often in bad weather, and there was no reason to think he'd gotten to the beach.

What an image we present, I said to myself as we started our walk toward Peters Pond, Satan having duly pooped and the bag with his offering having been deposited in the special container for such things at the entrance to the beach. The little Frenchie scurrying around at the water's edge, looking for mussels, crab legs, or shells that looked good to eat, his shore dinner, as Heidi and I call it; the wonderfully dignified Feng wearing his running shoes and otherwise the picture of Asiatic propriety in pressed khakis, a dark shirt, and a cotton jacket with many pockets, in one of which, I was sure, nested his Glock, loaded and ready to go; and I, taller than Feng, but hardly more intimidating in terms of easy-to-guess-at muscular mass, barefoot, in L.L. Bean shorts and an aged red polo shirt. My switchblade was in my shorts pocket. In my other pocket I had a box with Satan's treats. Around my neck a dog whistle hung on a lanyard. I used it rarely and was proud of Satan's response to one or at most two short blasts. Even if he was with other dogs, with a face so expressive of regret that my heart melted in sympathy, he would race toward me and a well-deserved biscuit.

I would have said something about this to Feng, but he spoke first.

This is a very beautiful place, sir, he said. It makes me long for the bay of Hong Kong and for the Beidaihe Beach in the PRC. That too is a beautiful, wide, and sandy beach. I went there as a child, before my father was disgraced during the Cultural Revolution. I'll never see the bay again, sir, or that beach.

I'm very sorry, Feng, I replied. I should have said something about Hong Kong. Of course, I haven't ever seen Beidaihe.

Very few foreigners have, sir. He smiled.

But I think one of these days you'll be able to go back. Your difficulties with the PRC authorities are by now old stuff, aren't they?

They are, sir, but memories in China are long. I was told to stop the investigation and I didn't. I couldn't. It wasn't only corruption, sir; it was a brutal and cruel murder of a girl. A high official. The girl was a bar girl. He thought he could do what he wanted. After my investigation, he was convicted by a Hong Kong court, and I will never be forgiven.

What could I say? Only the obvious banality.

I'm sorry, I said, but I'm sure you did what was right.

Then I added, Just as I know I was right to go after Abner Brown. I'm paying for it. But now I want desperately for this to stop, to be able to come to this beach again like in the old days, carefree and happy. It's just a wish. Like the proverb, Feng—if wishes were horses, beggars would ride. I don't expect it to come true. There must be a saying like that in Chinese.

Feng was silent for a while, his head bowed. Then he told me that no, he didn't think there was a similar saying in Chinese. It may be because of Confucian influence, he continued, that our proverbs concern people making an effort, and succeeding or not succeeding, and the reasons for the outcome. There isn't much space in China for wishes. I know a proverb, sir, that you might enjoy: The grand ambitions of a swan are beyond the comprehension of the lowly, who do not dare to dream.

IX

An indescribable weariness came upon me as we returned from the beach. I told Feng I was going to lie down and close my eyes for half an hour or so.

Very good, sir, he answered. I'll take care of the telephone and Satan's six o'clock walk. Have a good rest!

Oh, I'll be up long before six, I told him, and I'd like to take Satan out then. It drives me nuts to think I can't take my dog out for a stroll in the back streets of Sag Harbor. And don't worry: I'll have the switchblade in my pocket and the Colt in my waistband.

Feng knew better than to argue. He bowed respectfully and withdrew.

I lay down on the studio couch, just as my uncle Harry had before Slobo entered and tormented and killed him and his beloved Burmese tomcat. What moved me to choose that particular place to rest? Defiance, I suppose. I wasn't going to let memories of Abner Brown's hit men determine how I lived in my own house, any more than I would allow the Monster's miasmic omnipresence and threats to deprive me of my freedom to go about and carry on with my life as I pleased. Fancying that I had thrown down my gauntlet was very well, but dreams of Abner, his scarlet face as he read the file I told him I would be delivering to the U.S. attorney, and of the face of the Monster as I imagined it, unformed and therefore perhaps more terrifying, signified one thing only. Deep inside me I knew that the challenge I'd issued had been taken up. There was no going back.

It's rare for me to sweat, but I woke with my shirt and walking shorts soaked through. It was seven-thirty. Way past the hour at which we had accustomed Satan to have his evening walk. I urinated in the studio bathroom, washed my face with cold water, and went into the kitchen. The ingredients of dinner were on the counter, neatly arranged in little bowls; Satan, curled up in the Queen Anne wing chair, gave no sign of having noticed my arrival; Feng was on the telephone, speaking Chinese. At least he did not ignore me.

Putting his hand over the receiver, he said, I'm speaking to my colleagues in HK, sir. Satan has been out and has done his business. Dinner can be ready in half an hour.

Don't let me disturb you, Feng. Let's have it in an hour, or later, if you like. No rush. I overslept.

When I came down after my bath, the table was set in the dining room; Feng was still in the kitchen, as well as Satan, still in his wing chair.

May I serve you a drink, sir? Feng asked. A martini?

Yes, please.

He brought it into the living room, together with a bowl of prawn crackers that he knew were my favorites. I asked him to get a drink for himself—of course, he refused, saying he'd have some rice wine before going to bed—and to take a seat in the armchair catty-corner from mine. This he accepted.

What have you learned? I asked.

It's bad, as bad as I thought, or worse. They are depraved people, Yellow Flower, depraved without honor. Like leeches, sir. They attach themselves and don't let go.

Feng's diction never stopped surprising me. I had not imagined that "depraved" was in his vocabulary, but there it was, brought out so naturally. Or perhaps it was his HK colleagues who had said the word in English. Or had they used a Chinese expression that sent him to his Chinese-English dictionary? It didn't matter. He was fabulous.

Then what do you, or you and your friends, think Mr. Krohn should do? I asked.

They think Yellow Flower can't work in the U.S. They couldn't get visas. Soon someone working for them in America will get in touch with Mr. Michael Krohn. Most probably by telephone. He should record the conversation if possible or take careful notes on how much they want to be paid and how the payment must be organized. They think it would be very dangerous to refuse payment even if Mr. Michael Krohn has very good security. These people would strike. If not next week, then next month or later than that, and they may strike Mr. Michael himself or Mrs. Michael Krohn or Mr. Jonathan Krohn or his wife. It would not have to be the little boy. Or they may strike more than one person.

And the police?

If Mr. Krohn has police protection, perhaps the police will be able to catch the people working with Yellow Flower here. Perhaps HK or Macao police will pursue Yellow Flower. That will take time and it is uncertain. Sir, this is very dangerous.

All right, I said, can dinner wait while we call Mr. Krohn? If it can, I'd like to have you on the telephone with me to tell him exactly what you have told me. And I would very much like another martini.

It turned out that the dinner could wait, and I could have my martini. I called Jon Krohn on his burner—he had sent me a text message with the telephone number—and got no answer. He hadn't gotten used to having it in his pocket, I guessed, and I called him on his regular landline and told him Feng and I would like to speak to him on his other line. He understood what I meant and said he'd be ready. They'd finished dinner, and he'd take the call in his office. We spoke to him minutes later, or rather Feng repeated his advice.

There hasn't been any move from the other side, Jon said finally. What do we do?

Wait for the move, sir, replied Feng, and, while you wait, please be very careful. There should be security where Mr. Michael and his wife and the little boy sleep, and there should be security where you and Mrs. Krohn sleep, and during the day each of you should be under watch by security.

Right, said Jon. We have enough people, I think. They're all retired Mossad agents and police detectives. They're armed. And I've a call in to McCabe, the deputy director of the Bureau. Do you think you, Mr. Feng, and Jack could stop by tomorrow? Perhaps have lunch with us, and check out our arrangements?

I raised my hand and nodded vigorously.

Captain Dana says we can do that, sir.

Then we'll see you tomorrow, around twelve.

Can I just have a word with Mr. Krohn? I asked.

Feng gave me the receiver and I said, Heidi doesn't know anything about Michael's problem, I mean the casino, the threats, and so forth?

No, we haven't told her. Are we wrong?

I think you're right, there's nothing to be gained by spooking her while she's hard at work in Tokyo. But you should make very sure that the security you have for her is on the job, and on high alert.

How Feng had found time to prepare the dinner he served—stir-fried beef with leeks and hot peppers—was beyond me. Perhaps he'd prepared the vegetables in the city and brought them with us. I knew better than to ask. The kitchen was his domain and its secrets were not for sharing. However he had accomplished it, the result was delicious and, once again, I couldn't help admiring the sureness with which he matched the beef with a California Syrah he'd found in Harry's cellar and, for that matter, Harry's choice of wines to put down both in Sag Harbor and in the wine storage in the city. How oddly coincidences worked out. Feng had come to work for me on the recommendation of Martin Sweeney, the retired New York City detective whom I'd hired to do some sleuthing while I was still battling Abner Brown. He—

and his wife and daughter!—grew concerned that I wouldn't be able to manage on my own after one of Abner's thugs had beaten and badly injured Jeanette, Harry's old-time house-keeper who had stayed on with me, and Feng seemed to him the ideal replacement. That Feng would one day save my life did not surprise Martin. But how could Martin or I have fore-seen that it would be Feng's cuisine that lured Heidi to what turned out to be a series of dinners at my apartment during which I fell in love with her and she, little by little, began to forget that she was not physically attracted to men? Until now, when perhaps if asked point-blank, she would say that she had come to return my feelings? Or that she would bring into my life Satan, who was at that very moment stretched out alongside my chair, making strange French-bulldog noises that were his running commentary on current affairs while he patiently waited for dinner to be over and for me to move onto the sofa that was the perfect place for him to sit down beside me.

You're a lucky Frenchie, I told him, once we were comfort-ably installed and Feng had brought my coffee. You live in nice places with people who think you're a great guy. And if there is such a thing as deserving your luck, you deserve it. I used to think I was lucky too, but now I wonder if my luck isn't running out. I'm in deep shit, Satan, and I don't know what to do about it. Don't you worry too much, though. If anything happens to me, you've got Heidi, and if anything happens to Heidi, you've got Feng, and if anything happens to him there is Kenny, who would love to have you come to live with him.

Kenny was a back-elevator man in our building who I was convinced came to the kitchen—the elevator door opened directly into it—for the sole purpose of playing with Satan. All of the staff in the building had a crush on Satan, but Kenny was the one I felt sure the little Frenchie could count on. That was a sad commentary, I said to myself immediately, on my own utter loneliness. I had no family. And, somehow, I felt that if neither Heidi nor I nor Feng were there, it was not Jon or Helen Krohn who'd take in Satan. Helen would find twenty reasons for saying no.

Maudlin reflections, I told myself. Luckily Satan doesn't understand every word of this. But he knows you're sad, and that's making him sad too.

Feng appeared at this moment, summoned by the gods of whiskey, and asked whether I would like an Oban before turning in.

How did you guess? I asked, and I was overcome by equally maudlin gratitude when he appeared bearing a glass of what looked like a double ration of the marvelous stuff.

The idea of going to bed atypically early had been tempting me, and I would have probably acted on it, taking the glass upstairs with me and asking Feng to turn out the lights when he turned in, if the telephone hadn't rung. It was Heidi's cell phone. Our standard operating procedure was for her to call me, rather than for me to place the call. The weirdness of the time zone difference—Tokyo is thirteen hours ahead of New York—added to the varying demands of her work schedule convinced us that this was the best way to get to talk when she was alone.

Great news, Captain, she said. The Koreans have made a settlement offer no one in his or her right mind could refuse. The big boss, Mr. Tanaka, told me first thing this morning to accept. I called my distinguished opponent, Mr. Piggott, QC. He's a charmer, but this was one time he couldn't help sounding pissed off, and we agreed he'd email the papers formalizing the offer for me to review by the end of the day. If everything goes as I expect, I'll be at JFK on Wednesday and we can get an early start on our Memorial Day weekend. What do you think about that? I can tell you I'm in seventh heaven. This is a great result for the client and a great reward for Heidi Krohn, Esquire, who longs to show off her new pajamas to a certain former marine infantryman.

What do I think? I think I've just upgraded from seventh to eighth heaven. Let me know the flight number and I'll be there, certainly with your pal Satan and, if it turns out we can go directly to Sag Harbor, with Shao-Feng.

I told her then about Satan's most recent exploits, the weather in Sag Harbor, the progress of my novel, and all the while I was saying to myself, This adorable fool has no idea of the terror that will face her when she returns. Shouldn't there be some reason I could dream up to keep her in the Orient, away from East Hampton and Sag Harbor and New York? But there was no clever lie I could come up with, and I knew that if I told her the truth she would be on the first plane to JFK and to hell with reviewing the settlement papers.

I finished my whiskey and made a note to let Jon Krohn know about Heidi's new travel plans—she might have decided to surprise her parents by returning sooner than expected—so that he could give appropriate instructions to his security people. There seemed little point in alerting Joe Edwards. I'd no doubts about his integrity or his being solidly in Heidi's and my corner, but if Texas influences could make themselves felt in the organization, perhaps it was just as well not to pass on information he hadn't asked for.

As always before going to bed, I checked emails on my clean computer. A good-night message from Heidi, a good half of it consisting of emojis, to which I replied in kind, knowing they never failed to make her giggle. The rest—recommendations from the American Kennel Club for products indispensable to Satan's welfare, requests for money from assorted cultural institutions, and alerts from Nancy Pelosi, countless other Democratic Party functionaries, and Bernie Sanders—I deleted unread. My new novel, as much of it as I had written, way too little in my opinion, was still there when I opened Word. I would have liked to give it a tummy rub of the sort I had just given to Satan. Since that was a function not yet available from Microsoft or Apple, I contented myself with saving it once again, for good measure, and sending the new segment to the Gmail address at which I store my drafts.

I should have continued to the kitchen to say good night to Feng and perhaps pour a finger more of whiskey into my glass, but the habit I loathed drew me to Monster Land, my invaded, polluted laptop.

Since I had shut it down before leaving the city, it took a long moment to wake up. Ah, yes. The cobra icon was there, between Google and *The Guardian,* and it was writhing. With a sick taste forming in my mouth, I clicked on it. The website opened. "1 message," written in red, appeared in the mailbox icon. Once again, I clicked and read:

> The trap is set, fuckhead! For you and the Jewish slut.
> There will be no mercy. Tremble, for the end is near.

I snapped a photo of the screen and clicked on the message. Yes, a dialogue box came up in which I could type an answer. I lacked the self-control needed to ponder what I should say. Instead, the thought What difference can it make? flashed through my mind. I typed:

> It's your end that's near, asshole. I'm tired of you. Crawl
> out from your spider hole and talk to me. I want to
> know what's in your sick head.

There was no reason that such a thing could not be, and yet, when I heard his laughter—high pitched and maniacal, so different from Abner Brown's guffaws—I was astonished and, I must confess, shaken. Since his choice of words, his diction, were like Abner's, shouldn't he sound like Abner as well? That too made no difference. It was as though the Monster were right there in the room with me, and at once I realized that if he could broadcast sound to me, he almost certainly could hear everything that was said within the laptop's earshot if the device was open. I wished Joe Edwards had warned me about that. But here was an opportunity to test the hypothesis and, perhaps, finally engage this creature in a conversation.

You're whinnying! I guess you find the suggestion amusing. So, how about it? Who are you? What are you after? What have I done to get you on my back? How do I get you to go away and stay away?

I should add that, exhibiting presence of mind that even the most sadistic and demanding of my infantry-school instructors would have found commendable, I had turned on the Voice Memos function of my cell phone. Involuntary recollection of how my uncle Harry—by pure accident, I've always assumed, since he was taking a nap—recorded on his iPhone the irruption into his studio of Slobo, the hit man who murdered him? Or was it the speed-of-light, unfailing reflexes of a former Marine Infantry Force Recon platoon leader? In the face of this mission! Lord knows I preferred ten times over to be leading my men on a patrol to wipe out Talibans holed up on some Helmand hillside, the very one, if need be, where I took the sniper's bullet that ended my military career. Anything but the present nightmare.

The gurgling sound that issued from my laptop was not inconsistent with the Monster's clearing his throat and spitting, or perhaps silencing another fit of laughter. Then I heard him speak. His voice was high pitched, not unlike his laughter, and he spoke with what could be a slight foreign accent I didn't recognize or some sort of affectation.

Where are your brains, fuckhead? Those fucking Yale and Oxford brains? Or your memory? Or your second-rate novelist's imagination? Try to think! Try to imagine! Pain. Pain. Endless pain. Abandoned. Salvation. Return to life. More pain. Robbed of one love. By whom, fuckhead, by whom?

I've already told you, fuckhead, when I saw your baby pictures that I'm sorry for you, I said. So, you're really Abner's twin. What a murderous shit he was! Killed my uncle. Killed a woman I loved. He needed to die. But you, what kind of asshole are you? He wrecked you in your mother's womb. You should thank me for getting rid of him. Now go back where you came from, Monster, or I'll find you and kill you too!

As I uttered those words I realized they were stupid and probably counterproductive. But my brain seemed addled. I could think of no others.

More laughter, more gurgling, and then he shrieked: You're a stupid blowhard. You'll never find me, you'll never escape. I'm everywhere and nowhere.

After a pause, he spoke again: You don't understand anything, fuckhead: (a) I loved Abner, (b) I like to kill, (c) I like to maim, (d) I like to torture. The way I was tortured. I begged to be taught to kill, to be allowed to kill. The first time I killed, I killed my mother. The bitch who'd abandoned me. Abner himself led me to her. I cut her throat with kitchen scissors, and snipped off her nipples, those nipples my lips had never touched. It made me come to cut them off. That's when I became his killer. Always ready. Let him have the money and let me kill. Only he gave me money too. More than I could count. I like to watch when my people kill and torture. Or maim. Like that Judas couple in Westchester. What we did to them was beautiful. I watched and came and came and came.

For a minute or so, there was only the sound of labored breathing, more terrifying than his speech.

He shrieked again: Rejoice, fuckhead! Just thinking of what we'll do to you and the Jewish slut made me come. So delicious! You come in her mouth? Perhaps I will. Perhaps I won't kill you. It will be worse for you to be alive.

The website went dark. I stayed still for some minutes. Then I checked the Voice Memos on my phone. The recording was there. It wasn't just a bad dream. The photos I'd taken were right there too. A few minutes past eleven. It wasn't too late to call Joe Edwards on his cell phone, or Scott Prentice. I called Joe first, got him right away, and asked him to conference in Scott. I was afraid I'd drop one or the other if I tried to patch them together myself. Once they were both on, I told them briefly what had happened and had Joe explain to me how to email the recording to them. I knew how to send the photos. We agreed to talk again in half an hour.

Scott originated the call and spoke first.

This is worse than anything I could have imagined, he said. You're in deep shit with your Monster and, quite frankly, I don't know how we track him down. Perhaps Joe has some ideas.

I don't, not right now, Joe replied. One thing I can get the tech guys to test is whether there is something about this voice exchange that makes it traceable. I doubt it.

I do too, said Scott. About the only useful thing that's come into my head is this: the Monster pretty much says he was Abner Brown's killer. Let's take him down a peg: one of his killers. Perhaps reserved for special occasions. He may have actually been in on the Lathrop massacre. The agency has had an intense interest in Abner's criminal activities, including violent crimes, and perhaps I can use that hook to get our people on the case. What about you, Joe? Do you think this rises to the level of an overt threat sufficient for the Bureau to take action? A threat made over the Internet? I mean, to protect Jack and Heidi?

It should, sir. But as the captain knows, there are complications.

Well, let's hope you can cut through them. Let me know if you'd like me to weigh in.

Yes, sir.

All right, Scott continued, my advice to you, Jack, is that you become really, really careful. It may be that this fellow or his killers will make a mistake and give you, give us, an opening. More likely these are professionals who won't fool around. You don't want to fall into their hands or have that happen to Heidi.

No, I said, certainly not.

We said good night. I went to the kitchen thinking I'd bring Feng up-to-date and have another whiskey. He wasn't there. Must have gone to bed, I concluded. That's what I should do too.

The bottle of Oban was on the pantry counter. I poured myself a double shot and went about turning out the lights. Feng had set the alarm, I noted before climbing the stairs. Once in my bedroom, I got the Colt out of my duffel bag, put a bullet in the chamber, and laid the weapon carefully under my bed, where I could reach it in a quick swoop. I would have liked to call Heidi. But what could I tell her? That I was good and scared and didn't know which I wished more, that she were here, at my side, or that she'd stay away, as far away as possible?

X

We'll take Satan to the Krohns' lunch, I told Feng the next morning. They have two miniature poodles. Heidi says he has fun with them. Anyway, I don't like leaving him here alone.

When we were setting out, I asked Feng to drive. He likes to drive, and I know that the way I drive—although I consider myself an excellent driver and have never been in an accident—makes him nervous. We're like an old married couple, I thought, my Chinese housekeeper and me. He nags and tells me to be careful, and I do my best to humor him.

About halfway to East Hampton on Route 114, Feng asked permission to speak about my conversation with the Monster. He'd listened to it in the kitchen on my cell phone before we left the house and told me that he rerecorded it afterward on a separate device.

It's to be sure we have it preserved, sir, he explained, if anything happened to your phone.

Nothing like an old professional, I said to myself. He's

right. Routine and more routine. Police work and more police work!

Of course, Feng, I replied. I'd very much like to hear what you think. Please be very frank, and don't worry about making me feel bad if you think I handled it badly.

Sir, I believe your first guess was right. This person is very likely Abner Brown's twin. Even if he isn't Mr. Abner Brown's twin, it seems that Mr. Brown took care of him. Helped him in some ways. That would be why he is grateful and loved him. When those feelings are present together, they can be very strong. It also seems that this person is insane. If that is true, sir, it would be better to treat this person with respect. Please forgive me for saying that. You shouldn't insult him even if he uses insulting language when he addresses you. We were always told at the training wing in HK that scolding crazy people doesn't work.

He fell silent. After a while I asked whether that was all.

Yes, sir.

Thank you, Feng, thank you very much. That's a useful lesson. I'll keep it in mind and do my best to follow it.

The gate in the wall surrounding the Krohns' estate was shut. A black Range Rover was parked to the right of it. Two heavyset fellows in black fatigues got out. One of them took a leisurely look at Feng, and then came to my side of the car. I lowered the window.

Your name? He spoke with a rough accent that, having been told the composition of the Krohn Enterprises security group, I thought might be Israeli.

Jack Dana. And that is Mr. Feng. Feng Houzhi. Mr. Krohn
expects us.

Check the trunk?

You bet.

The other guy raised the tailgate and, to my surprise, actually opened and verified the spare tire and tool compartment.

He took something out of his pocket that looked like a TV
remote and pointed it at the gate. It opened.

Good to go. Proceed to the big house. Someone will park
your vehicle.

The guards must have called ahead. Jon Krohn met us at
the front door of his huge Italianate residence, one that con-
tained, as I had learned from the tour I was given when Heidi
first brought me to lunch with her parents, fifteen bedrooms,
two living rooms, a library, a sunroom, a media room the purpose of which I didn't fully grasp, a thirty-seat movie theater,
a gym with an adjoining sauna, and a wine cellar stocked with
amazing vintages of great wines.

A perfect weekend hideaway—she had giggled—for a couple that hardly ever entertains and never has houseguests!

After effusive and lengthy expressions of gratitude for my
help and moral support, and for taking the time to come to
lunch, which Heidi had told him was the last thing a working
writer ever wanted to do, Jon said he'd like to take us for a
walk around the grounds so that Mr. Feng could familiarize
himself with the layout. He was especially eager to hear what
he thought of the security arrangements.

Jack, he continued, turning to me, excuse me, but please
not a word about any of this at lunch. Neither Helen nor Lilly

has any idea of what's going on. They realize that Michael is very upset about something, but he's a man of many moods. They tend to take them for granted.

The six superbly planted acres could not fail to dazzle, even if one had seen other grand Hampton estates. Jon pointed out successively smaller replicas of the main house: two guesthouses (one of which was occupied by Michael, Lilly, Jonjon, and Jonjon's nanny), the servants' quarters, and the two four-car garages with living quarters upstairs, one of which had been turned into a guardhouse. The security personnel had the use of the apartments above the guardhouse and, when needed, the one above the other garage.

How many of these men have you got here now? I asked.

Ten or twelve, he answered. The number fluctuates a little. They work in six-hour shifts. Five are supposed to be always on duty. You told me, Jack, not in so many words, that I should pull out all the stops. I think it's too many, don't you? The place is walled, except on the ocean side. There is an electric wire along the top of the wall. If you trip it, an alarm goes off. There's a fence concealed in the dune, and it too is electrified. A very low charge, of course, just enough to set off the alarm if you climb over it. Have we done enough? What more can we do? Mr. Feng, what do you think? You're a professional and, Jack says, a hell of a good one.

Thank you, sir. We saw the two men at the gate. What are the other men doing?

Some are watching the TV screens. I should have said we have surveillance cameras going in all directions. I'm not sure of their placement, but they're there.

That seems very complete, sir. My one suggestion would be that someone should keep particular, full-time watch over Mr. Michael Krohn and Mr. Jonjon Krohn.

I read you, replied Jon. But that means we have to tell everything to Helen, that's my wife, and Lilly, that's Michael's wife. They'll go stark raving mad. Let's think this through. For the moment, let me show you the rest of this place.

We followed him past the cutting and vegetable gardens, the five-lane Olympic pool, the baby wading pool, the two tennis courts, and the basketball court.

We're a basketball family, he told us, perhaps noticing my expression of surprise. Michael and I like to shoot hoops. Even Miss Heidi joins in. By the way, she's pretty good. And now, let's walk toward the beach. After all, that's what makes this place worthwhile.

His mood had noticeably lightened. He was clearly proud of all of his property, but the beach with his own private access was his crown jewel. I knew from Heidi that he bought the place some years before she was born from the estate of the nonagenarian last living member of an old New York family, tore down everything that was on it, and created his own version of an Italian village.

The dune along the ocean side of the property was overgrown by rugosa roses that were already in bloom. Jon pointed out the chain-link fence he had mentioned concealed in the growth. A winding path had been cut through the roses to sturdy wooden stairs leading to the beach below. At the top of the stairs, in the opening in the fence, was a gate, on the beach side of which was a sign: PRIVATE PROPERTY—KEEP OUT.

The gate is electrified too, Jon said. If we lock it, whoever wants to come in from the beach has to punch in a code. If he forces the gate open or manages to climb over it, he sets off an alarm heard in the guardhouse. Oh, and there is a surveillance camera—Jon pointed—so that the guys in the guardhouse can know what's going on. Do you approve, Mr. Feng?

It's a very professional system, sir.

Thank you, Mr. Feng.

Feng's face remained pleasantly bland, his usual expression.

Whether or not Jon was satisfied with this response—he did not ask for a confirmation from me—he walked us down the steps onto the sand, gestured to the east and then to the west, and said, This is paradise. The best beach in the world, and, believe me, I've seen all the good ones. Just take it in! Such a gorgeous Sunday in May, and there is nobody here, not as far as the eye can see! Our neighbors have access, just as we do, but entre nous they don't use the beach a whole lot. They're seldom here. Sometimes, during school vacation, you will see kids and grandkids. Surfing. It's a pretty good place for beginners. If you don't have private access, Mr. Feng, and you want to go to the beach here, you have to have a beach sticker, which is available to East Hampton residents at a reasonable price. Don't ask me, though, what it is! If you have a sticker you can park at town beaches. The Two Mile Hollow Beach a couple of miles this way—he pointed again to the west—or at Indian Wells Beach, which is practically in Amagansett. You'd think people from those beaches would walk over here, but they hardly ever do. Not even in August. Probably because those town beaches themselves aren't crowded. People don't feel any need to move.

Satan and the poodles had followed us and were now gamboling at the edge of the water, the more enterprising of the poodles rushing in when the surf receded. Satan followed, but fortunately knew enough to stop and hurry back to safety when the water level reached his chest.

I'd better get him, I told Jon. Frenchies can't swim. It's the great sorrow of his life. Heidi gets into a panic when he starts thinking that he can play in the water with the other dogs.

Jon laughed. Don't worry, Satan looks as though he knows what he's doing.

I'll put him on the leash, sir, said Feng. That may be safer so early in the season, before he gets used to the beach again.

That's a very good man, Jon said as soon as Feng was out of earshot.

I nodded. Very much so. Heidi and I are lucky to have him.

Jack, there was another call from these Chinese enforcers. About an hour ago. Michael says he recorded it. I haven't verified whether he really did. The guy speaking to him, the usual guy, said the price is now twenty million. Michael claims that he kept his cool and asked how the money should be paid. The guy's answer was that the problem was now out of his hands; it has been referred to another organization; and Michael was going to regret not paying his debt to the casino when it was due. Really regret it. And bang, the guy hung up. Jack, what are we going to do? Twenty million is a lot of money, but right now I'd gladly pay it! What should we do?

Have you spoken to the FBI—to Mr. McCabe?

First thing this morning. He referred me to someone in the transnational organized-crime group concentrating on Asia, a fellow with a Chinese name or maybe a Korean name. Ben Liu. Nice guy, very sympathetic, said they'd get right on the case and gave me his direct number and the number of his assistant.

Well, that's good. Is there any reason we shouldn't tell Feng about all this? I keep him filled in.

That's fine, if you think that's best.

I do. And here he is, with the dogs.

What I think you should do for now, I continued, is to do what Feng has already told you: in essence, have one of your security guys never leave Jonjon's side. Someone should keep watch over Michael and Lilly as well. And someone should specifically guard the house they're living in. Let's see what else Feng has to say.

I gave Feng a summary of what Jon had told me. His face, normally impassive, seemed graver than usual.

You're right, sir, about keeping watch over the little boy and the parents. Mr. and Mrs. Krohn should be watched over also. If there is another organization, probably an American gang, they may have new ideas. Also, manpower.

Do you think, Mr. Feng, that our arrangements are adequate?

There was a note of desperation in his voice. He didn't seem to realize that he was going around in circles, that the question had been put and answered.

Have the people who work on your estate, sir, gardeners

and others like them, been subject to background checks? I think they should be, and that only people who have been checked should be allowed to enter.

Of course, you're right, Mr. Feng. How stupid that none of us has thought of it. I'll have that put into effect at once. And other than that?

Other than that, sir, I think your arrangements are good. Your people should be on high alert. Do they know precisely what is happening? If they don't, I think you should inform them in order to make them understand the urgency and ask that they keep what you tell them to themselves. I am very glad that the FBI will help. I am afraid that I believe Mrs. Krohn senior and Mrs. Krohn junior should be told of the danger and of the need to take precautions.

Jon and Helen Krohn's and my efforts to persuade Feng to have lunch with us and the younger Krohns proved unavailing. He insisted on having a quick bite in the kitchen. Afterward, if Mr. Krohn gave his permission, he would like to take another walk around the property and perhaps chat with the security people.

For my part, I failed to get Jon to agree that we would discuss the situation openly at lunch, once Jonjon and his nurse had left the table.

I just can't do it, Jack, he told me, shaking his head. The women will have hysterics, and Michael will say I've betrayed him. That's what he'll believe. He has no sense of responsibility. Let me do it my way. First, I'll talk to Michael and give

him a chance to tell his story privately to Lilly. I'll speak to
Helen quietly as soon as Michael and Lilly have had their
talk. God help us!

I shrugged. There was no use arguing. But seeing that he
expected me to speak, I shrugged again and said, Please try
to get these conversations done quickly. There is no telling
when or how these people will move against you.

We sat down to lunch on the open veranda in back of the
house, overlooking the beach. I could not have imagined a
more idyllic setting in which to drink rosé champagne and
eat oysters followed by cold poached salmon, couscous salad,
and a strawberry mousse. I didn't like Helen much, and my
impression of her didn't improve as I listened to her per-
orate about Donald Trump, whom she knew personally and
respected as a businessman and for being the best friend
Israel had ever had. The president was then in Saudi Ara-
bia, or perhaps had already left and landed in Tel Aviv, and
she didn't doubt that between him and Jared they'd come up
with a deal that all parties would buy into. I kept my mouth
shut. It was just as well, if my silence gave Lilly the impetus
to open hers. It turned out that she was a shiksa who hadn't
converted—in glaring contrast to that adorable Trump girl,
she cried gleefully—with views about illegal settlements on
the West Bank, the hardships of the daily life of West Bank
Palestinians, and so forth, which led her to a resounding conclusion: If Trump were a friend to Israel, he'd lean on Bibi to
give the Palestinians full citizenship rights within Israel and
a real homeland on the West Bank. Instead, he is teaching

Israelis to betray their humanitarian and democratic roots. Helen turned red. For a moment, I thought she was going to get up from the table and make a scene before she left.

Jon must have had the same idea because he said in a loud and firm voice, Lilly and Helen, we have a guest here, Jack Dana. A goy, for Christ's sake! Let's talk about him and Heidi, and what we can do to give them a very good time during the Memorial Day weekend. I recommend a dinner with our old friends and whatever young friends of Heidi's and Jack's happen to be in the Hamptons on Sunday night. With a small and discreet band playing Cole Porter! Dancing in the sunroom. We'll take up the rugs. What do you think, Jack?

A brilliant idea, sir. With your permission, I'll ask Heidi what she thinks when we talk this evening.

He laughed. I see she's trained you well. Do ask her and let Helen and me know the answer. You might even suggest she give her old father and mother a call!

I made a mental note that I must tell Heidi to tell her father that we don't want any such entertainment. What was Jon thinking of? In the present circumstances, the idea of throwing a big party at his and Helen's place was insane.

Helen didn't open her mouth during the rest of the lunch except to urge Jonjon, who was seated on her left, to eat what was on his plate. Lilly knew she'd won a skirmish, if not a battle, and was clearly enjoying herself. She said she'd read all my books and proceeded to prove it by discussing them with attention to details she wouldn't have been likely to have noted in reviews and remembered. I'd be lying if I denied that I was pleased. Appearances, of course, are misleading, but she didn't look or act like a bookish sort, and she lived in Hong Kong, which is not exactly the Athens of Asia. That could mean only one thing: my books were getting around.

I told a lie—that I didn't drink coffee these days because I had trouble sleeping—and took my leave as soon as coffee was served.

Jon accompanied me to the front door, squeezed my arm, and said, Thank you, forgive us. When Helen gets on the subject of Israel, she really loses it. Trump as Israel's best friend! As my grandfather of blessed memory used to say, with friends like, that who needs enemies? Anyway, once again, thank you! Let's talk before the end of the day.

I don't want to be a bore, I replied, but you aren't treating your problem with the seriousness it requires. Helen and Lilly must be told, members of your security should follow Jonjon and Michael wherever they go, and I think the same goes for you and Helen.

I found Feng trying, without much success, to teach Satan to fetch a rubber bone.

Let's go home, fellows, I said.

As we pulled out of the driveway, I added, That was really something. Satan and you, Feng, should rest. I too need a rest, but I should do some work.

Yes, sir, Feng replied. After some minutes of what felt like constrained silence, he continued: If you don't mind my doing so, sir, I would like to point out that the security at Mr. and Mrs. Krohn's house should be better. The personnel is good, the men are experienced, but it would be useful to explain to them the danger. Perhaps there should be several more men. The wire along the top of the wall, and on the dune, is important, but skilled intruders could avoid tripping it. That is why it is probably essential to patrol along the perimeter during the day and especially at night. On foot or in those electric carts that are parked near their quarters.

I said, You're surely right. I'll tell Mr. Krohn that this is your opinion when we get home. He may well want to talk to you about it. The difficult question will be, I think, who should speak to the men. Mr. Krohn? Perhaps you? Should one gather the men and talk to them as a group or explain the situation to the head of security, and let him take it from there? I tend to favor talking to the head guy, but perhaps I'm wrong.

Feng made no comment.

Well, let's think about it and speak again when we get home, I said. Wouldn't it be nice if, for a change, there were no new developments?

If there were developments, they were not apparent. The house in Sag Harbor looked as beautiful as ever and undisturbed. I shooed Satan out into the garden, where, wasting no time, he resumed his principal Long Island occupation, the hunt for chipmunks and voles. Feng announced that he was going shopping for dinner. It seemed that a further conversation with him about security at the Krohns' would have to wait. I followed Satan and saw that he had spotted a chipmunk under the steps leading into the study.

Good boy, I told him. Make sure he doesn't get away.

Sasha Evans was in her garden on the other side of the fence between our properties, weeding her vegetable patch. She scolded me for not having let her know I would be in Sag Harbor. As it was, she had an invitation to go out to dinner that evening. Boring people, she confessed. It would have been more fun for the two of us to have dinner together. But if you live alone, you end up accepting invitations even when you know you shouldn't.

This weekend's trip was a last-minute decision, I told her, but I'll be coming a lot now, with Heidi.

So that's a deal, she said. Next time you're here, dinner *chez moi.*

Inside the study, my clean laptop reposed on the worktable side by side with the laptop the Monster had polluted. I didn't try to resist. It had to be done: I opened the polluted machine and logged in. The cobra icon began its vibrations. I clicked and read:

Hello, roadkill! The trap has snapped. By coincidence, I've got you exactly where I want you. Have a nice afternoon! There won't be many of them.

Roadkill. I no longer remembered whether it was Abner Brown himself or his thugs who called me that or dead meat, but I realized that now, faced with the Monster, I missed them. They were creatures of flesh and blood. They dealt on terms I understood. Abner's thugs tried to shoot or knife me; I could give as good and mostly better than I got. Abner was

someone I could beard in his Houston lair. With the help of
Kerry and later Heidi I could construct a dossier sufficient
to send him up the river for life or, as it happened, drive
him to suicide. But this ubiquitous malevolent and macabre
absence—how was I to defend against it, let alone attack?
Under the message there was a space for a reply. I decided
not to take the bait. What would be the point of continuing
the exchange of insults?

So long as my infected laptop was turned on, he could
doubtless eavesdrop on me. I shut the machine down and
called Joe Edwards and then Scott to describe the visit to the
Krohns and the Monster's latest message.

Joe, I asked him, do you think the Bureau is on the Krohns'
case? I sure hope so. Feng doesn't seem all that impressed by
their security arrangements, and I can't say that I am either.

There was a silence. Then I heard him sigh deeply.

I don't know, I really don't know, sir, he said finally. The
Bureau isn't what it used to be. Information doesn't flow the
way it used to. Things that were done as a matter of course
aren't done or are done in a direction that's different from
what you expected. I'll see whether I can nudge people.

Understood, I told him. Thanks, and keep me posted if you
can.

Scott said he had to call me back, which he did within a half
hour, which I spent, quite unable to work, watching Satan
check out every square foot of the garden. Every few minutes, he'd trot back to me. His look left no doubt about his
feelings: utter frustration. The chipmunks always got away.

They're too fast for you, I told him. Nothing you can do about it. That's just the way it is. Like squirrels, always zooming up a tree.

Scott's mood was grim after I told him my story, including the part that concerned Joe.

This is awful, he said. You're in danger. I know you think you can take care of yourself, and that's mostly true, and there's no one better than Feng, but whoever this Monster is, whatever he represents, that's all beyond calculation. I'm trying to get the Agency into the act, and I've some hope of succeeding. But right now my advice to you and to the Krohns would be to go back to the city, to your nice apartments that are ever so much easier to guard than these houses in the Hamptons. The Krohns—every one of them—should make sure they don't take a step outdoors without a bodyguard or two at their side. I suppose the old man has a limo and a chauffeur he knows and trusts. Let him use it. Or use his other cars or rented cars driven by his security people. One driving, one riding shotgun.

They won't do it, brother, I replied. The weather's great, they've got the kid here, Memorial Day weekend is coming. . . . Don't forget Jon Krohn is a multibillionaire. Those guys may sound much of the time like reasonable people, but deep down they think they're omnipotent and invulnerable. Ordinary rules don't apply.

Well, if they want to be assholes that's their problem.

Right. And you're dealing with one more asshole, Scott, your old pal Jack. Heidi's getting back from Tokyo on Wednesday. I want to bring her out here for the weekend, and she's *d'accord*. We need a few days of good weather, playing with the dog in the garden, walking on the beach.

I see, Scott replied slowly. You're stupider than I'd ever imagined.

XI

Her Nippon Airways flight was early. At the gate at 12:20, instead of 12:45. The luggage appeared on the carrousel in a jiffy—those Japanese airlines are whizzes at it, she told me—she had one of those trusted traveler cards that let her zoom through passport control, and at 1:10 she was in my arms, lithe and warm, smelling so sweet I thought my heart stopped beating. She was wearing the best-cut Mao suit I'd ever seen, the only one I'd ever seen made of beige shantung, and burgundy-red suede loafers. A matching pocketbook swung from her shoulder. She'd traveled in business class—I think she or Kerry told me that lawyers no longer got to fly in first class even on very long trips like Tokyo to New York City—and she must have changed before leaving the plane. How else could she have attained such exquisite freshness of face, hands, and attire?

This is the most beautiful suit, I told her, and I don't think I know it. A perfect outfit for travel.

You haven't lost your eye for clothes, Captain. She laughed.

You can't know this outfit because I had it whipped up in Hong Kong. And it's not especially for travel: it's for arrival and finding myself in your arms. And that's not all I acquired in Hong Kong. There are those pajamas that I'm very eager to model. For guess who!

Darling, I said, after I'd hailed a porter and given him her suitcase and a prodigiously heavy and ugly black leather item that I knew was a litigation bag holding her documents, Feng is waiting a little way off in the car. We've brought your blue jeans and country shirts and, if you're not too tired, we could go straight to the country. What do you think?

It's a dreamy idea, she answered, except for this.

She pointed to the litigation bag.

I should really get it to my office, to my secretary. Everything is neatly arranged inside. She'll be able to send stuff out and do the housekeeping before the long weekend. Do you think that's possible? I could call her and ask her to have the bag picked up from somewhere here, but there are all those signed documents in it. I'd hate to have something go wrong.

It will be no trouble at all to drop it off, I said. Feng will be delighted. If you're hungry, we can also have a bite to eat in the city while we're at it.

No, she wasn't hungry, and she didn't want to keep Feng and, perhaps more important, Satan waiting while we had a sandwich, so Feng handed the bag to her firm's mailroom messenger who, summoned by a phone call, was waiting on the sidewalk when we pulled up at her building, and got back on the FDR and the Triborough. Once we were on the bridge, she turned to look at the Manhattan skyline, glimmering in the early afternoon sun, and said, I'm so happy! I'm happy to be with you, I'm happy to see my city, I'm happy to be going to your beautiful house. I want to see my parents' beautiful house, and I want to see my lovely little Jonjon and take him to the beach! It's so wonderful that he's there! It makes having Papa and Mommy there almost bearable. Do you think someday we could have a little Jack?

I swallowed hard. What could I say at such a moment?

Normally, Satan rode in the back of the station wagon, behind a barrier Feng and I had installed when we discovered his propensity to climb into the front seat and insist on putting his paws on the steering wheel. This time, because I knew how Heidi had missed him, we let the Frenchie travel in the back seat, in her lap, until, fully convinced that she was back and loved him as much as ever, he fell asleep, his happiness documented by bulldog harrumphs. Then Heidi and I cuddled—her expression for lovemaking that stopped short of possession—while Feng impassively kept his eyes on the road until she too sank into slumber. When happy and relaxed, Heidi often snored just a little. Not quite like Satan, except for the occasional crescendo. A sound that made me feel I had come as close as I ever would to Nirvana.

Feng must have heard that happy little noise as well and concluded that he could speak without worrying that he would wake her up.

Forgive me, sir, he said, I try not to listen to conversations that don't concern me or my service, but I believe that you have not explained to Miss Heidi the situation with the Monster or the attack Mr. and Mrs. Krohn's family is under. Perhaps I shouldn't be saying this, but I believe she must understand the situation in order to be appropriately prudent.

I hope that I blushed. He made me feel truly ashamed of my weakness.

Of course, you're right, Feng, I answered, please don't apologize, please never hesitate to tell me when I'm grossly stupid. You're right. You're one hundred percent right. It has to be done, but I was too weak, too happy to see that she was happy to be back, to do the right thing. I'll speak to her soon after she wakes up. You'll hear what I say. Please break in if you think you should add anything or correct anything in what I tell her.

She opened first one eye and then the other just as we left the Grand Central Parkway and turned south to pick up the Long Island Expressway. The traffic was dense, probably because people were getting an early start on the Memorial Day weekend. I figured it would be an hour and a half before we reached Sag Harbor.

Oh, what a good sleep, she said, stretching. A wonderful sleep. A promise of things to come. But I'm so thirsty! You wouldn't have some water with you, Feng dear?

Heidi really liked him, and he really liked her. It was a standing joke for her and me, with a big dollop of truth in it: His cuisine won her heart. I was just lucky enough to be his employer.

Would Miss Heidi like a cup of good hot black coffee? I

have milk if she'd prefer to have milk in it. I also have hot green tea and some little sandwiches.

She wanted black coffee, as did I, and we both fell upon his smoked-salmon and smoked-trout sandwiches.

Wow, she said, after wiping her mouth on a tea napkin that was included with the provisions in Feng's hamper, wow! Do you think we can have some of your braised duck soon? Perhaps tomorrow night?

Nothing could be easier, Feng answered.

Well, she said, now I'm ready for news. Jack, tell me everything that has been going on. You haven't told me how your book is coming along. I really do want to know.

She sensed that I'd drawn back instinctively, and said, Please, Jack! I've been away for weeks. I really need to know.

All right, I said. Some of what has happened is downright awful. But you're right. You absolutely need to know. And look, Feng is aware of everything. So I hope you don't mind if I ask him to jump in and correct what I say if he thinks a correction is needed.

Sure, she replied, sure, please do so, Feng.

She clutched my hand and looked up at me. There was fear in her eyes, a look I'd not seen before.

She'd read in the press online accounts of the Lathrops' murder, and she knew it was still unsolved and that there had been no mention of clues having been found. But that was all, and I plunged into the dreary recital of having been invited to view the carnage at the scene of the massacre, the eruption on my computer screen of the Monster, my suspicions about his link to Abner Brown that were turning into certainty, the buildup of his vile threats that now included her, and the new and separate menace hanging over her family and Jonjon. . . .

I'll murder Michael, she wailed.

Your father may beat you to it.

Instantly I regretted this attempt at humor, but she disregarded it. Perhaps she hadn't heard me. She was crying. This too was new. She was the bravest of girls, the lawyer warrior who when I tangled with Abner had insisted on being at my side and had narrowly escaped being killed.

Satan had never heard her cry either. He too began a sort of keening—a noise that wasn't barking as when a stranger was at the door, or a frenzied sort of yapping when Feng undertook to take hold of my computer case, which Satan considered my important personal asset. The Frenchie was weeping.

Heidi caressed him until he'd quieted down and asked Feng whether there was any coffee left. There was another cup.

We also have some cognac, he volunteered. Would Miss Heidi like a sip?

She had a big sip, sat up straight, and asked: What are we going to do, Jack? What's going to happen to Jonjon, to us?

I know only one thing, sweetie, I said. Somehow, we will endure. How we're going to defend ourselves, how we're going to defeat the Monster, how I'm going to kill him, I don't know. We have to see his next move. Killing him may be impossible. It may be just as impossible to hand him over to the police. And we won't know how to deal with the extortionists pursuing Michael until they tell him where and how to send the money. As you know, the FBI is on the case. Twenty million is a lot of cash to put into the hands of criminals, and probably the Bureau will say don't give them a cent. That's the standard line, I believe, and, as you surely know better than I, it's the right one in the context of law enforcement. But in this case I for one will say to your father, Pay and pay fast! What do you think, Feng?

I believe that the captain is right, Miss Heidi. These gangsters are vicious.

I had told Mary Murphy that Heidi and I were coming out for the weekend on Wednesday, and, although it wasn't her day to work at the house, she was there to welcome Heidi. She had put flowers on the kitchen table, on the dining room table, and in the master bedroom. On the kitchen counter, there was a baking pan of chocolate brownies, cut into little squares. Mary was acquainted with the marvels of Feng's cuisine, but clearly she thought that an American snack or dessert was what Heidi needed after traipsing around in the Far East. Some ten minutes later Sasha appeared. She too wanted to welcome Heidi, and she too had a present for her, an aquarelle of our house.

Will you come to dinner? Heidi exclaimed. Friday evening? For something special that Feng will dream up?

She was studying the painting and the inscription—FOR BEAUTIFUL HEIDI WHO IS MAKING JACK SO HAPPY—and made no effort to hide the tears that were running down her cheeks. I too was on the verge of tears. Mary had opened the house. The smells of a garden in full bloom under a May afternoon sun filled it. The house and the garden were beautiful. The furniture gleamed, much of it Dana family pieces that Harry had inherited from his parents and I had inherited from mine and moved here. Mary liked antiques and took delight in waxing them. Yes, everything was as I wished it to be—if only the Monster would vanish like a bad dream, if only we were allowed to bask in our happiness.

Feng prepared one of Heidi's favorite meals that evening. Cold sesame noodles, pork *shumai* dumplings, braised duck, and stir-fried string beans. Having the braised duck already this evening was a surprise, he said, for Miss Heidi. We drank slightly chilled Chinon, had sliced pineapple for dessert, and abandoned the Chinon to finish the meal with double espressos and sixteen-year-old Oban.

Heidi asked whether I'd rather she wore her new white or red pajamas to start our night together.

Black, I told her. Black as the darkest night.

We cuddled for a long time, and then she told me, Jack, take me, take me, take me. I've wanted you so much.

It's impossible to describe total happiness, but that is what I thought we had achieved when, after we'd both come, she whispered, Jack, I had my IUD taken out before I left for Hong Kong. I so want us to make a baby!

I woke much earlier than she but remained in bed, fearful of disturbing her if I got up, luxuriating in the warmth of her body and the sound of her breathing. Occasionally, she snored a little. From time to time, she uttered the little squeaks that I took to be signs of recollected pleasure. Her breath was fresh, her skin was clear, she had actually said she wanted a baby! We had traveled a long way since the evening almost four years earlier when we met for dinner at my favorite Italian restaurant on Madison Avenue to figure out why Kerry, her best friend and my girl until she threw me over, had been killed just then—we were both sure that she had been murdered—and how to avenge her.

She opened her eyes finally, looked around, rubbed her eyes, and exclaimed, So it's true! I'm in bed with my sweetheart, I'm in Sag Harbor, USA, at eight-thirty Eastern Daylight Savings Time, I'm not in Hong Kong, I'm not in Tokyo, and I talked my way out of going to Seoul! Hooray for Heidi! Can Heidi have breakfast? Please, Captain Jack, pretty please!

I told her that not only could she have breakfast, she could have breakfast in bed, served by me.

When I went down to the kitchen, I found that Feng had anticipated Heidi's wishes. Breakfast for two was ready on the tray, with plain yogurt for her and a cut-up apple, a thermos of what I knew would be very strong and extremely hot coffee, and *The New York Times*. There was no arguing with Feng. He insisted on carrying the tray upstairs, set it down on the little Federal table outside the master bedroom door, and tactfully withdrew. I knocked, found that Heidi had changed into white pajamas and was sitting in bed, propped up on the pillows, grinning as though she'd swallowed a canary.

She was ravenous, she said, let the *Times* wait. Having made short work of the yogurt and company, and downed two cups of coffee, she made a little moue I understood—she wanted me to move the tray from the bed—and opened her arms.

Jack, she said, I want you. I don't want a bath, I don't want to get dressed. I want you. Inside me.

Afterward, she asked, Do you think it could have worked? Last night and this morning? I'm so ignorant. I had a sort of period after the doctor took the coil out, but nothing since, and I've lost count of days. Can you get pregnant right away?

I don't know, sweetie, I told her, but I sort of think you can. I hope you can. Let's just keep working on it!

Later, after she had had her bath, which she asked me to watch, she said, I really must call my mother. I said I would, first thing in the morning. That's all right. I'll tell her I slept late. Would you be an angel and bring the phone?

I went back to the bedroom while she talked to her mother, but I couldn't help overhearing her laughter or her promise that she would be in East Hampton in plenty of time for lunch—but only on condition that Jonjon would be at table with the grown-ups.

It can't be helped, I thought. Of course, she wants to see her parents and her nephew, and she knows the situation her family is in and the separate danger to which she and I are exposed. Jon Krohn understands the threat that hangs over Jonjon very well, all the billionaire bullshit notwithstanding. All that can be done is to be very vigilant.

I went downstairs while she was still on the phone and called Jon on his burner.

Jon, I said, I just heard Heidi make a plan to go to see you and to have lunch. I've told her everything, so in theory she understands the risks. Will you please get your security detail energized? I know I can't prevent this visit, that I mustn't even try to prevent it, but it makes me very nervous.

Understood, he told me. You can count on me. But I don't see how we're to go on. Heidi will want to return to the office, to work, to carry on as usual. What should we do? In Paris, during those terrorist attacks at supermarkets, people hide in meat coolers. We can't do that, or can we?

No, I said, you can't. My mantra is: Be careful. The rest we have to make up day by day.

When Heidi appeared in her freshly pressed khakis and white shirt and gleaming white Converse sneakers, I realized that I was blessed beyond any deserving.

You're unspeakably glamorous, I told her. And I love you unspeakably much.

It's mutual, Captain, she replied, but the question is whether you love me enough to stay here like a good boy while I run over to East Hampton and visit my aged parents. You're welcome to come along and have lunch with the family, but something tells me you'd rather work.

You may go, I said, if you let Feng drive you over, wait for you, and bring you back, and if you let him watch over you. You know the danger. I want him to watch over you. He's a very smart man, Heidi, you know that, devoted to us, very tough, and very, very reliable.

I was afraid she'd protest. After all, she was a big girl, had a black belt in karate, and I'd forgotten what else, but she said, I'd love to have Feng drive me. We'll decide together on the menu for the weekend and for next week in the city. And we'll leave you Satan.

In fact, I didn't get down to work as soon as they drove off. It was time for Satan's midday walk. I couldn't go with him to the ocean beach because Heidi and Feng had taken the car, but we went to the very end of the Long Wharf and made our way back along the Upper Sag Harbor Cove all the way to Otter Pond, at which point we turned toward home.

I fed Satan, whose rapid gait had been a sign of growing hunger, told him he was a very good dog, and enjoined him to answer the telephone and write down messages. That was our standing joke. As for me, I told him, I was ducking out to the American Hotel for a lobster BLT. Disgustingly rich, I added, but that's all right. Unlike you, I've been losing weight.

With a sigh and a nod to the absent Feng, I locked the front door and armed all the alarms and, with *The New Yorker* tucked under my arm, set off to the hotel. For a Thursday before Memorial Day, the restaurant wasn't crowded, and it made no difference that I had forgotten to make a reservation. The maître d'hôtel was glad to see me, as was the waiter who, for reasons I had never plumbed, insisted on speaking to me in French. A great feeling of peace descended on me, as though this were a sanctuary that the Monster could not violate. I have never been a beer drinker, but I liked the new Montauk craft ale, and sipped it with growing pleasure. The BLT took just enough time to appear to confirm that it had been made to order, the crisp bacon included, and was as good as I had remembered. The latte I ordered to finish the meal scalded my lips, my idea of how coffee should be served.

I looked at my watch. One-thirty. Heidi didn't seem to be suffering from jet lag. She should be back before three. A walk with Satan on Gibson Lane beach might appeal to her, and I might even be able to convince Feng that he didn't need to escort us. But she might prefer to take a nap. That is what I would vote for, provided we could take that nap together. I paid the bill, shook hands with the French-speaking waiter, the maître d'hôtel, and the manager and promised each to be back soon. Yielding to a sudden craving, instead of going home I walked toward the harbor and got a rum-raisin ice-cream sugar cone. It was perfect. Eating it contentedly I finally doubled back and headed for the house and Satan, who, I supposed, by now was missing me. Just as I passed the American Hotel again, my burner cell phone rang. Feng. I slid the slide to answer and said, Hello, Feng, is everything in order? When do you expect to be back home?

Sir, he answered, excuse me, something terrible has happened. They have seized her, Miss Heidi, and the little boy.

What do you mean? Where are you?

I'm in the car, sir, driving toward the house. I should be there in less than half an hour. The gangsters, sir, I think the ones who have been threatening Mr. Michael Krohn. They've seized Miss Heidi and the little boy. Please, sir, let me explain to you what happened as soon as I get home.

His voice kept breaking up. I couldn't be sure whether it was because the connection was bad on that stretch of Route 114, where I supposed he was, or because he was crying.

All right, I said. I'll wait for you at the house. Drive carefully. Don't get caught speeding.

I should call Jon Krohn immediately, I thought.

No answer. I kept walking as fast as I could now without breaking into double time and tried again. Still no answer.

The house was undisturbed. I let Satan out into the garden and sat down in the kitchen to wait for Feng. Once again, I called Jon's burner. Still no answer. I tried the landline and got voice mail. It seemed absurd to leave a message. I called the burner again and this time left a message, asking Jon to call back as soon as he could. Then I stood by the window, waiting. A few minutes later the Volvo pulled up in front of the house. I rushed to the front door and told Feng not to bother putting the car into the garage.

Come in, for Christ's sake, I shouted, and tell me what happened.

They have seized Miss Heidi and the little boy, he said again, they have seized them.

What do you mean, Feng, I asked, who seized them? How could it be?

The story came out, related methodically, in Feng's precise and sometimes stilted manner. The drive to East Hampton was a very pleasant drive. Miss Heidi drove, quite rapidly. The guards at the gate waved them through. At the main residence, the entire Krohn family was lined up at the front door. The little boy jumped into Miss Heidi's arms. She hugged and kissed him and kissed her parents and Mr. Michael Krohn and his wife. When she put the little boy on the ground, he pouted and would not let go of her hand. Then Mr. and Mrs. Krohn said that everybody would have drinks on the back terrace and very kindly invited Feng to join them. Feng accepted, in part because he wanted to have another look at the terrace and the lawn sloping down to the dune. Mr. and Mrs. Krohn again very kindly invited him to join the family at lunch. This time he refused, explaining that he should have a quick bite with the security people and discuss with them their current arrangements. Mr. Krohn agreed and said this was a good idea and offered to walk over to the guardhouse with him. Since they were alone, Feng permitted himself to say to Mr. Krohn that it might be good if Mr. Krohn put in a word for him with the supervisor—he feared that the guards, all of them former intelligence agents or law-enforcement personnel, felt some resentment or embarrassment at his second-guessing them. Once again, Mr. Krohn was understanding and must have spoken persuasively with the supervisor because, after Mr. Krohn left, the security people treated Feng well, as though he were one of them.

They went over the security around the perimeter, especially at night. Everything seemed in order, and the supervisor suggested that they all have a bite to eat at the picnic table outside. The Krohns' kitchen had sent over a tray of sandwiches and pitchers of iced tea and lemonade. They were eating when suddenly they heard an anguished shouting from the guardhouse. In the TV camera room, the man on duty, a former New York Police Department detective, was shouting, An attack, an attack, and pointing at one of the TV screens. On it they saw two figures, one large and one small, Miss Heidi and the boy on the beach at the foot of the stairs surrounded by four figures—men in black combat fatigues and face masks—seizing Miss Heidi and the little boy and carrying them into the surf, which was low, and onto a large speedboat that had suddenly appeared in the camera's field of vision. Miss Heidi was struggling hard, but she was completely overpowered. In a matter of seconds, Miss Heidi, the boy, and the men were all on the speedboat, which drove south rapidly, out of sight of the camera.

The supervisor sounded a general alarm and reported to the FBI at the number that Mr. Krohn had been given by his contact at the Bureau. The supervisor also called the Coast Guard and the local police. Then we looked at the digital video preserved by the beach-surveillance camera. It showed Miss Heidi and the little boy running down the steps to the sand, throwing a Frisbee, and then the figures of men rushing out of the rugosa roses on the dune. That is where they had been hiding. In the dune. They did not cross the perimeter wire, and therefore did not set off the alarm. The defect in the security was the absence of personnel guarding the beach perimeter, reliance on the wire inside the dune, and lack of attention to the possibility of an attack from outside the perimeter.

I have failed you, sir, Feng concluded. You told me to watch over Miss Heidi, and I foolishly left her side. I have failed you.

XII

don't know how long I sat with my elbows on the kitchen table, my head between my hands. At one point, Feng offered me tea. I waved it away and muttered, Bourbon. One bourbon. Another bourbon. It was no use.

Sir, Feng said, it might be useful to call Mr. Joe Edwards and Mr. Scott Prentice.

You're right, I replied, and did nothing.

Then my burner rang. It was Jon Krohn.

You know, Jack, of course, you know what happened. You warned me, and I didn't pay attention. I didn't call you earlier because the place is crawling with FBI agents and policemen. A fat lot of good they will do. They can't find a trace of the speedboat! The helicopter search, zero; Coast Guard, zero. Vanished! Then maybe ten minutes ago, I got a text message on my phone. Not Michael, but me. Let me read it to you:

If you want to see your grandson alive again you will send fifty million dollars in Bitcoin to the following—there follows a long chain of figures—the transfer to be received not later than midnight tomorrow. Don't fuck around. Send the money, or the kid is dead!

Jack, what should I do?

Have you showed this to the FBI guys?

Yes, they said don't do it, it's an opening gambit, give us time, we'll find them and get your grandson and daughter back.

Nonsense, I answered. Pay! This is bad stuff. Can you raise that kind of money on that schedule and pay it in Bitcoin? I must tell you, I don't know how that's done.

I do know something about it, because we've made payments in Bitcoin in Asia. And I can get the money. I've a line of credit at a Swiss bank. They're six hours ahead of us. I'll call the banker I deal with at seven in the morning his time and make sure he gets it done. But, Jack, they haven't told me how we get Jonjon back! And they didn't mention Heidi.

That'll be the next step. I think they'll tell you once the transfer of Bitcoin is completed. They didn't mention Heidi because they took her only because she was there, on the beach. Anyway, it's our only hope. If they weren't giving Heidi back, they'd have named a separate price.

Thank you, Jack, I think you're right. I wish I had listened to you before.

Good luck! And please call me as soon as the transfer of Bitcoin takes place. I don't care what time it is.

I couldn't think of anything I could do beyond calling Joe Edwards, who had already heard the news. We talked in a desultory fashion and then, just as I thought we were going to hang up, he said, Excuse me for sharing with you a hunch, Captain. I've got no basis for it, but I think that you had better be extra-careful yourself. I'll keep an eye on all the information coming in from the field and keep you posted.

Next, I faced Scott's icy fury. You couldn't take advice, could you? Why, why didn't you do what I told you to do? Why couldn't you and the Krohns go back to the city and make it that much harder for these bastards to pull their stunt?

All right, I answered, you were right, and I was stupid. Have you any suggestions now?

None. Though I've got to hand you this: you were right to tell your father-in-law-to-be to pay without haggling and without delay. Let's hope the kidnappers live up to their part of the bargain. The FBI is on the case full force. I wish I could get the Agency into the act, but I need a pretext. So far, I haven't got one.

Jon called at a quarter of four in the morning. Quarter of ten in Zurich. I was in my study, reading on the sofa, dozing off intermittently. Satan was stretched out by my side, making deep bulldog noises. Poor guy, I thought. His happy life may have come to an end too.

It's done, Jon said. The banker said he could watch the money on the Bitcoin exchange going into those bastards' wallet. Don't ask me how he watched or what he calls their wallet. It's clear they have the fifty million. What do we do now?

We wait, Jon, we wait. If we can, we pray.

This will kill Helen. She took a sleeping pill strong enough to knock out a horse, but she's awake. Crying, Jack, crying.

Michael and Lilly are here, in the main house, in the library. They haven't even tried to go to sleep. Lilly's face is blank. A white blank. I think she'll leave him as soon as we get the kid back.

I wouldn't blame her, I replied.

Immediately, I was sorry, but Jon didn't take offense. I wouldn't either, he said. I want to get Jonjon back. He and Heidi are my life. Once they're back, I'll figure out how I keep Jonjon and show Michael the door.

We'll stay in touch, I told him. The first one to have news calls.

I got up to urinate and afterward, out of what had become a bothersome habit, checked my iPhone to see what new horror or stupidity our malevolent president had sprung on the world. He was still in Europe and apparently had kept quiet since yesterday's outburst about prosecuting leakers of intelligence information. On the other hand, there was news about Jared: the first son-in-law was under FBI investigation for allegedly proposing in the postelection period to establish a secret back channel for communicating with Russia.

One more screwup, I said to myself. The trouble is that no one will hold him or Trump to account for this stuff.

Then, still out of habit, I opened my polluted laptop. The cobra icon was doing a belly dance. Terrified, I clicked on it and read:

I told you, nice coincidence? Don't you agree now?
The Jewish slut and the Jewish brat! I've got them both
under lock and key, and I've got you where I want you.

You didn't realize that debt collection is my sideline? How would you, with your head up your ass? Profitable, when the deadbeat has a billionaire father like Jon Krohn. The father has paid up, so I'll give the brat back. Alive and in one piece. He'd have paid one hundred million, if I'd told him to, but I charge reasonable prices. The slut is something else. I never said I'd give her back. Guess what: he didn't ask for her. So, what shall I do with her? I can deliver her to my boys. They'd have fun before we kill her. Kill her very slowly. But I have a better idea. Maybe I'll let the boys fuck the slut first, yes, up her ass would be nice, but nothing more than that. When they finish, I'll let her and the brat go, but on one condition: in exchange I want you. There is a lot I want to do to you. That is my choice. What is your choice, hotshot?

As I was taking a picture of the message, a dialogue box appeared below it. I guess I wasn't quick enough, because the Monster added to his text:

What's the answer, shithead?

I typed in it:

You can have me if you deliver the boy and Heidi safe and unharmed. Promise that no one will lay a finger on her, that you won't give her to your men.

The response came:

I promise.

I typed:

All right, you can have me. Where will you deliver Heidi and the boy and when?

He answered:

I thought that's what you'd say, asshole! You know why? Because you have no choice! Tonight, at midnight. An exchange. I deliver them, and I take you. You come alone and unarmed. No funny tricks, no surveillance. You try it, I'll detect it, and I'll kill the kid. And my men will fuck the shit out of the slut before we kill her. If you do as I say, we'll take you and leave your sweetheart and the kid intact. Whoever wants to pick them up can do so at fifteen after midnight. I get a hard-on just thinking about what I'll do to you!

Where, Monster, where?

The location will be given you on this site at 23:15. Remember: come alone with no bullshit business, or the slut and the kid die.

I photographed it all before the website went dark. What use would the images be? I had no idea.

So that was that. In some strange way, I wasn't surprised.

I'd played a game I didn't understand and hadn't asked to play. No wonder I'd lost. Lives end, one way or another. Even if they end very badly, they end. That was my ultimate shield. It had been that to my marines, mangled beyond recognition, their guts ripped apart by an IED. It had been that to Harry, tortured by Slobo, and to the Lathrops, tortured and butchered by the Monster's thugs. The immediate task was to take the next steps without putting Heidi and the boy in even greater danger. One thing seemed clear: I had to keep the FBI and whatever other forces of order were crawling around the Krohns' place from interfering. I had no doubt the Monster would detect any attempt that was made to follow me to my rendezvous and any trap set for him or his thugs, and he'd make good on his threats. He'd kill the kid, and I was sure what he'd do to Heidi wouldn't be euthanasia. So mum was the word. But I had to tell Feng. A sort of loyalty led me to decide I had to tell Joe Edwards and Scott as well. I could count on their brains and common sense. They'd understand I had to go through with the Monster's program. Telling them gave me, incidentally, a chance to say goodbye. But my first order of business would be getting hold of Moses Cohen and making arrangements for—what else could I call it?—my absence.

As usual, he was at his office at nine o'clock sharp in the morning, and the receptionist put me right through.

Moses, I said, skipping the usual preliminaries, I have something of an emergency. First, can you tell me whether in my current will I take care of Feng?

Let me look.

After a short pause, he told me, Yes, you do. You leave him five hundred thousand. That seemed to both of us handsome.

It still does, I replied. Now here is the emergency. I'm about to do something that may turn out to be dangerous, and if I survive, it may be only after a prolonged period during which it isn't known whether I'm alive or dead. No, please don't protest, I have no choice. What I want is to give Heidi and Feng, acting individually and separately, a general power of attorney to do whatever they think right with my property. Obviously, I'm most concerned with paying salaries, including Feng's, and all bills like maintenance in New York, insurance, and so on, but I want it to be much broader. Can that be done? A power that will be good if I disappear and it isn't known whether I'm alive or dead?

Yes, it can. You want me to shut up about not doing whatever it is you plan to do?

Yes, please shut up, and help me to get this done and in effect before you go home this afternoon.

Have you got access to a printer?

Of course.

In about forty-five minutes, I'll email to you the power of attorney. Read it. If you have questions, call me. If it's OK, print it, sign it, get your signature witnessed and notarized. Send the document to me by FedEx at my office and email me the tracking number. And could you call me or email me after it has all been done?

Yes, and I can't thank you enough for this and everything you've done in the past.

I was glad to have these mechanical tasks to accomplish.

Telling Feng wasn't easy. He listened carefully to what I had to do that evening, and to my leaving him and Heidi in charge of everything, and said, I hope, sir, that this will not turn out as badly as we think.

I do too. If it does turn out badly, please take good care of Satan.

The conversation with Joe Edwards confirmed my high opinion of him.

I don't see what else you can do, sir, he told me. I'm not going to interfere, and I'll make sure the Bureau doesn't interfere and put Miss Krohn and the boy at risk. But I would like you to call me on the burner after you receive instructions as to where you're to go this evening. We have ways of possible satellite surveillance that no one can be aware of. U.S. government satellites are in constant orbit. It will be a question of zeroing in. What we learn may become useful.

Shitty fucking break, said Scott. I guess you've got to go through with this. I wish I could get to you in time to give you a hug before you go to wherever you're going. Will you please email those screenshots to me right away? Don't worry, I'm not thinking of any sort of helicopter raid. It would be bound to fail, even if I could get the Agency to authorize it. But there is tomorrow and the day after, and we will want to catch the Monster and bring him to justice or kill him.

I told him what Joe Edwards had said about possible satellite surveillance.

He's a good man. He thinks straight. I hope Heidi and the kid will be all right and that you'll survive this.

.   .   .

It was a little past noon by the time I'd sent off the power of attorney and finished the essential telephone conversations.

I'm going to take Satan for a walk on the beach, I told Feng. I think I can do it alone. Why should they go after me now when they know they'll have me this evening? We'll be back in time for his lunch, and after you've fed him, let's go out, you and I, for a good meal. Agreed?

Yes, sir.

In that case, I'll do one more thing first, Feng, before heading for the beach. I'll call Jon Krohn.

I got him on his burner and told him I was quite sure that he'd get Heidi and Jonjon back this evening, after midnight, at a place I didn't yet know. Feng would call him after eleven and tell him the location. Naturally, he wanted to know more. I said emphatically that was all I could say.

Now it was time for our walk. Beach! I told Satan. Car! Let's get the car! I said. We're going for our walk!

Following our ritual, I held out a treat, whereupon Satan leaped into the open back of the wagon. Inside he sat, like a good dog. I gave him first one treat and then another—giving him two treats for jumping into the car wasn't part of the deal, but did that matter?

It was an almost windless, sunny day, temperature hovering around sixty degrees. Satan did his business obligingly as soon as he got out of the car so that I could scoop up the mess and throw the baggie containing it into the dog-poop receptacle instead of carrying it until we returned to the parking area.

We walked west, close to the edge of the ocean. The sand was hard, interesting enough to Satan to sniff and dig happily, but without crab legs and broken shells that were dangerous for him to chew. He'd run ahead and turn his head to make sure I was following. When we got to the Main Beach, he sat and looked at me questioningly. Do we really have to keep going?

It was past one. Car, Satan, I called, time to go home!

This was what he had hoped to hear. We got to the car and home in record time, and contrary to custom I gave Satan his lunch myself.

A good lunch, Satan, I said. I hope you've enjoyed it.

Then I washed my hands and face, changed my shirt, and put on a tweed jacket. Feng was ready.

Let's walk over to the hotel, I said. We'll just waste time trying to park.

My last lunch, I said to myself. I wish this were Paris, and Satan could come to the restaurant with us. I'd already decided that I'd have dinner at home, one of those dinners that Feng knew how to throw together, and that would be my last supper. Immediately, I was ashamed of the self-pity and bombast.

Let's order, I said to Feng, and let's have a bottle of wine. Is white wine all right with you? Some sort of Pouilly-Fuissé? I plan to have oysters and crab cakes.

That was quite all right with Feng. Oysters weren't to his taste, and he took instead a lobster bisque, but crab cakes were right up his alley. He had perhaps a glass and a half of wine. I finished the bottle.

Satan was glad to see us when we got home. I sat in the

armchair in my study with Satan in my lap making especially loud contented noises. When Feng appeared unbidden, bringing me an Oban, I drank it gratefully. He stood calmly in the corner of the room until I had finished and said, May I suggest, sir, that you take a nice nap? I'll look after Satan and will have dinner ready at nine. It's a dinner that can wait, if you decide, sir, to sit down to dinner later.

I thanked Feng, thinking, This is a really good man, and lay down for my nap.

Bath before dinner. A long bath. I wasn't in a hurry. Dressed in clean khakis, I went into the living room to find, to my great pleasure, that Feng had made smoked-salmon canapés to accompany the martinis he served and that he had opened a bottle of Côtes du Rhône to accompany his very spicy stir-fried beef. The muscat grapes he'd bought were excellent. It was a quarter before eleven when he asked whether I'd like coffee.

Yes, I said, but could you first bring the Monster's laptop?

I put it on the dining room table and opened it. At eleven, the cobra came alive with a message:

Stand by!

All right. I went to the bathroom and urinated, took my driver's license out of my wallet, and put it in my trousers' pocket.

Here, I said, giving the wallet minus the driver's license to Feng. I won't be needing it.

Eleven-fifteen.

Go to Louse Point Beach. There we will give back the
slut and the kid and take you.

There was a reply box. I typed:

I'm on my way.

Feng, I said, Louse Point Beach. Please call Mr. Krohn
and tell him to be there at fifteen after midnight sharp to get
Heidi and Jonjon. No bullshit with police or they'll kill Heidi
and the kid. Please repeat that. Make sure he understands
and will follow instructions. Then call Joe Edwards and Scott
Prentice and tell them that's where I'm going and that they
want me there at midnight. And, goodbye, Shao-Feng! Thank
you for everything. I'll never stop being happy that you came
into my life.

Satan was at my feet. I caressed him, left the house, got
into the car, and drove off.

Louse Point. I'd been there years ago. Beyond Springs,
beyond Green River Cemetery, east of Barcelona Point. A
friend of Uncle Harry's, a rich photographer, had had a house
on the way to Barcelona Point. Going home at night she'd get
so scared of the road being blocked by bandits—that's what
she called them—and being robbed and raped that she'd make
a U-turn and go back to civilization to crash at a friend's.
Sometimes, at Harry's. Route 114 was deserted. I didn't think
the police were out to catch speeders and drunken drivers. I
stepped on the gas. Passed Springs. Turned north and passed
the cemetery. Louse Point Road. Ten minutes before mid-

night. I slowed down to a crawl. No point in being early. At three minutes before midnight I rolled into the beach parking lot and walked to the beach. A starry windless night. The Sound smooth and hostile. A shitty beach. Rough sand or pebbles. Never come here again. That made me laugh.

I don't know where they came from, but suddenly they were there, black-clad figures huddled together. They broke. Standing on the strand alone were two shapes I recognized. Heidi and Jonjon. He was holding her hand.

Heidi, I called out.

Had she heard me? Did she see me? Did she know? Could she understand? As the words left my lips, I lost consciousness. Was it an expert blow with a blackjack to the back of the head? An injection? I never found out.

Pain. Pain. Pain. Pain. Pain.

Endless pain? No. Death ends pain. Even before death comes, shock ends it.

Oh, but they were good at bringing me out of shock. Someone they called Dr. Bill administered the injections. It was he who inserted the tube through which they fed me for some weeks. When they broke my shins, it was also he who reset them, chortling that I'd be really bowlegged.

Just like me, just like me, screeched the Monster. And Dr. Bill kept my wounds clean. What is done to you, he'd say, is done for a purpose.

Remember the hooks fixed to the ceiling in Guantánamo interrogation rooms, the prisoner's hands, tied at the wrist, his arms stretched up as though in prayer because they are attached to the chain suspended from a hook? The prisoner stands on tiptoe as long as he can. When he weakens, the pain in his shoulder joints added to the sum total of all other pains inflicted on him is unbearable. That was the position I was in when I was whipped, when my back and buttocks were flayed, when a huge cobra, like the Monster's website icon, was etched with acid on my chest, when my face was rearranged, nose and cheekbones broken, teeth knocked out, all this, the Monster told me, to the end that I look like him.

Like my larger twin, he tittered.

With two exceptions, he did not torture me personally. I like to watch, he said, and watch he did, from the beginning of each session when I'd be attached to the ceiling hook like a side of beef, until the time when I was allowed to sink into a heap on the blood-, feces-, and urine-spattered floor, my hands tied behind my back, covered by one of the operators, as they referred to each other, or Dr. Bill, with a blanket. Don't get me wrong: the floor was hosed down, sometimes more than once a day, once I was hanging from the hook, but care was taken to ensure that when I finally lay down it was in my own blood and excrement.

Watch he did, the Monster seated in a leather club chair. Meals were brought to him on a tray. Porridge-like stuff, because he was toothless, just as I had become, and did not use, or perhaps couldn't use, dentures. Not infrequently, when what was done to me was particularly to his taste, he unzipped his trousers, took his penis in his hand, the palm of which he first smeared with Vaseline, and masturbated. He came noisily and licked the discharge from his hand. He hurt me with his own hands only toward the end. He told me then that the basic work had been done, but he had saved two procedures for himself. The first one was old-fashioned: with a kitchen spoon he plucked out my left eye, let it fall on the ground, crushed it under his foot, and, in mimicking a BBC accent, cried, Out, vile jelly!

The quotation put him into a fit of laughter. He shook and laughed and shook.

My own left eye was also ablated, he observed, once he had calmed down. For medical purposes, of course. This was for fun, and to complete the resemblance between us. Physical resemblance. Otherwise, zero. My intelligence is in the stratosphere. Higher than my beloved Abner's. You're a stupid fuck. Your good grades at Yale mean nothing. Grade inflation for well-born jocks. By the way, I've thought of castrating you. Not chemically, of course, or by cutting off your balls, but by crushing them. With pliers. Something I'd do personally. I've decided against it. Why? To maintain the resemblance between us. The surgeons fucking with me when I was a baby didn't castrate me. In fact, when they saw I had an undescended testicle, they performed the minor surgery required to make it join its colleague in my scrotum. So, you're minus your left eye and you're keeping your balls.

Blood was trickling down from my eye socket. I tasted and drank it. Did I scream when the Monster blinded me? Then or through the uncounted days that came before? I don't know. Sometimes I did, sometimes I was too tired to scream. I never tried to stifle my screams out of pride.

The next day, or some days later, I was suspended as usual. The Monster walked around me, examined the scars on my back and thighs, the curvature of my legs, my balls, the cobra on my chest, my toothless mouth, the empty orbit of my left eye.

Good job, he said. When you think that the work on me that turned me into what I am was spread over years. And we've accomplished this in no time at all. Three months! What do you think, fuckhead?

Why, I answered, why? Why have you done this to me? Why did you slaughter the Lathrops? I know you're insane. Is that the reason? Your only shitty reason?

You see what I mean? Where is your Yale- and Oxford-trained brain, fuckhead? Overrated. You had the answer at the start. It's because you hounded my sweet brother Abner to death. And you couldn't have done it without that whore Kerry, whom Abner told me to kill, or Judas Lathrop, could you? Abner told me to kill them too. I wish I'd done it while he was still alive. You asked me why I love Abner? Because when he found out what my mother had done to me, put me in an institution for malformed, handicapped, and retarded children, he forced her to let him get me out of there. He caressed me, he made me know he loved me, and took me to a school in Switzerland, near Gstaad, where they took care of me and educated me. Educated me, fuckhead! And Abner got the best surgeons to correct what the assholes in Texas had done! Those are the reasons, or what you and assholes like you call reasons. But no reason was needed to kill Judas Lathrop and his broad or to do all that I've done and will do to you. If you are bad, if you are like me, if you want to hurt and kill, doing evil is its own supreme reward. It's like breathing. Eating and drinking the foods and liquors you crave most. It's the most delicious of pleasures. When Abner realized I was really bad and wanted to do evil, to hurt and kill without anything that assholes like you call reasons, he said, Come and work with me! Be my other self. Already he was founding his black empire, and someone had to be at the head of its enforcers and extortionists and torturers and murderers. But first he put me to a test. He brought me to our mother's house and said, Show your stuff and kill her. I did! I did! I did! And I still run all the black empire. Killers for hire, extortion—that's what I like best—human trafficking, drugs, arms dealing, organs for sale from stock or harvested to order! Evasion of North Korean, Iranian, and Russian sanctions. A booming business! But what I like the best is dealing directly with clients like you! And what if I told you a useful secret? Being good is hard. Fuckheads like you have to be taught to be good. Hard work and teaching that don't always take. But you don't have to be taught to be bad or cruel or treacherous. You let yourself go and have fun! Great, glorious fun!

Once again, he laughed. I thought he'd never stop.

You forget that I know this disgusting story about your mother, you hyena, I said when he finally stopped. You posted it on your website. You're demented as well as criminally insane.

Forget that I've told how I did it? That I posted it? I never forget. I tell that story over and over and over and each time it's as though it were the first! And now, fuckhead, since you've been insolent, you will be punished.

No preparations were required. I was naked and in position. They used leather whips that cut the skin. I fainted or went into shock, and this time Dr. Bill did not wake me.

XIII

Count slowly to one hundred before you take off the blindfold, asshole. You touch it sooner, I kill you.

Was this a threat or a promise? I knew that voice. From sessions on the hook. On the electric bed. Fuck that shithead. He doesn't know that now more than ever it seems rich to die. I counted slowly and untied the cloth. Intolerable sunshine, so brilliant it blinded my remaining eye. The first daylight, first sunshine, since however long it was, since that day I gave myself up to the Monster. Shading my eye, I looked around. Manhattan, the Battery. How had I gotten here? Had they sedated me? I had no memory of anything since the session on the bed frame. That was some time after the whipping. Not too much time could have passed, though, because the wounds on my back and on my thighs still oozed some sort of gooey exudate. The Monster himself had turned up and lowered the current. It was worse than anything that I had yet experienced. I fainted, and I suppose the good Dr. Bill revived me.

The Monster had spoken: Say please, nice Mr. Monster, please no more, please no more today.

I remained silent.

He laughed, fiddled with the switches, and gave the knob a turn. The current hit my balls.

I screamed, Pretty please, pretty please, stop!

He laughed again and gave me another shot.

I must have passed out. When I came to, the Monster had been right there, having a drink.

Dom Pérignon, he said, I like to have over ice. Too bad you can't have any. The electric did wonders for your brain. You should have tried being polite sooner. Now it no longer matters. Pretty soon we will be saying so long, kiddo. I'm going to send you out into the great world so that you can discover the pleasures of life when you've been turned into a pale copy of me and have no Abner at your side. But no worries! I'll keep my Cyclops eye on you and make sure you'll never forget Abner or me. And now one more for the road. Ciao!

Was it possible that this time the pain had been even sharper? I can't tell, any more than I can tell what happened between the moment he administered the shock and when I awoke at the tip of Manhattan.

Carefully, tentatively, I got up on all fours. Then, even more slowly, I stood up. Really, that was some job they'd done breaking my legs and my feet. Staggering toward State Street, I wished I had a stick to lean on. My progress was so exhausting and so painful that every few steps I let myself down to the ground and rested. The street was empty. Early morning,

I figured, the sun being so low in the east. In the glass door of an office building on Whitehall I saw my reflection. A caricature of the Monster, dressed in rags: pieces of burlap sewn together or fastened with safety pins. The trousers had a pocket. It was empty. A homeless couple was asleep, huddled in the doorway of a Starbucks that had not yet opened. Was not this the solution: hunker down in some other doorway, under a bridge or in a subway entrance? Let it all end. I was so tired, in such pain, so ashamed of what I had been turned into. Why not sink into the Hades of homelessness and folly? My reverie, if one may call it that, was interrupted by the screeching tires of a taxi that didn't slow down sufficiently quickly to avoid knocking me down. I made no attempt to get up. It was too hard and pointless. Had I been hurt? I told the guy I had no idea. He helped me gently to my feet, swearing all the while about worthless bums and drunks.

I'm taking you to emergency at Bellevue, he told me.

He wore a green turban. Sikh, I supposed.

Don't, I said, I'm probably all right. I really need to go home. I have no money on me, but if you take me to where I live you'll get paid and you'll get a big tip.

I gave him the address.

You want to go to the Metropolitan Museum?

I want to go home. Up the avenue from the museum.

All right, let's go.

He got me into his cab, one of those cabs with sliding doors I didn't begin to have the strength to open. We were on the way.

Probably because there was no traffic, he didn't take the

FDR Drive. Broadway, then Third Avenue. Somewhere in the thirties, he turned west and took Park Avenue. I read the hour on the clock over Grand Central. Five after seven. At Eighty-Fifth Street, he turned west again and then south on Fifth Avenue and stopped at my building. Emil, the loquacious doorman I once thought might be the Monster's snitch, got up from his perch inside the entrance and ambled over to open the door of the taxi. Seeing me, he recoiled.

It's Mr. Dana, Emil, I managed to say. I know I don't look like myself. Please pay this nice driver and tip him fifty dollars. Let's go! What are you waiting for?

Yes, sir, Captain Dana, sir! He shook himself as though to wake from a dream and held out his hand to help me alight.

Thanks again, I called out to the driver.

The elevator man hadn't come on duty. I pressed the number for my floor and wondered whether Feng was awake and would hear the doorbell.

Careful, sir, careful, Feng warned me. Don't let Satan be rough with you. That was later, when I was seated on a chair in my bathroom.

When he had opened the front door, he said simply, Welcome home, sir! Perfect manners. He allowed no hint to show of shock or surprise or revulsion. Offering me his arm, on which I was glad to lean, he led me to the bedroom.

Would you like juice or tea, sir, before you have your bath?

Juice, please, Feng. Any kind of cold juice.

He appeared with a glass of orange juice on a silver tray so quickly that I hadn't had time to try to urinate.

I'll go to the bathroom first, I told him.

This would be the first time since May. I had been pissing and defecating under myself whether suspended or collapsed on the floor of the cell. Would I be able to piss now, as it were on command, into a toilet? My bladder was full, but I wasn't sure. I let my trousers fall and took aim. There was a period of hesitation, and then a normal flow. A bowel movement was coming on too. I sat down and although constipated relieved myself. A look at the toilet paper in my hand confirmed what I suspected: my rear end hadn't been cleaned since I didn't know when—unless being hosed with ice-cold water after the last whipping could be called a cleaning. My buttocks must be caked with feces. I'd take a bath, I thought, but first that orange juice.

I put on my trousers and sat down on the wooden chair in the bedroom. Feng would disinfect it. That was when Satan jumped into my lap.

I think he knows me, I said. How very strange! Through the stench.

Of course he knows you, sir. He has missed you very badly. Every night he sleeps across the door to this bedroom. He doesn't allow anyone, including Miss Heidi and me, to approach your desk in your study or sit in your place on the sofa in the library.

What a good boy, Satan, I said. You wouldn't have a treat I could give him?

Of course he did. In a plastic envelope he took out of his vest pocket.

Had I forgotten Heidi? Now that he had pronounced her name, I said, Really! And how is Miss Heidi? I asked.

Very well, sir. Very busy. She has a new job she will want to tell you about. This being Saturday, she is in East Hampton, at her parents'. She wanted to take Satan, but he lay down and wouldn't budge. He was waiting for you, sir!

Oh, I said, and thought, So it's Saturday. Another reason the streets were empty.

May I run a bath for you, sir?

Yes, please. I'm tired and not at all well. Oh, and this is a stupid question, but I really don't know anything. Am I right to think that Miss Heidi is living here?

No, sir, she has gone back to her apartment on Lexington Avenue, but she has left almost all of her things here. She told me it felt odd to live here without you. She comes a couple of times a week, though, to play with Satan and have a meal. She claims she can't get good Chinese food elsewhere.

And another stupid question. What is today's date?

Fourteenth of October, sir, 2017, Feng replied. You've been gone almost five months.

Almost five months! It's hard to believe that's how long they held me. And that I have endured it and survived. I would not have thought it possible. But then, think of the guys in Auschwitz. Or wherever Pol Pot kept them. Or in our own Guantánamo. Some guys held there now for fifteen years, perhaps longer. In Auschwitz and other German camps Jews and perhaps groups like queers and Gypsies were there on the way to the gas chamber. Others were worked

and starved to death. I don't know what went on in Cambo-
dia. But in Guantánamo the torture was to force the prison-
ers to reveal information. Anyway, that was the rationale. The
Monster tortured me for the sake of torturing. For fun. Ha!
Ha! Ha! Was that harder to endure? I had no idea.

And Heidi—it was surely a good thing she had moved out.
I mustn't let her near me. Not now. Perhaps never. I loved
her—that was the fixed notion in my head. But what did that
mean in my circumstances? The question Am I still capable
of love? was stupid. It mustn't be asked. But if it were asked,
could an answer be given? I wasn't sure. I wasn't sure I recognized myself—neither the image I saw in the mirror nor the
dull absence of feelings other than pain and fear of more pain.
Satan was OK. Warm and strong and so alive. Feng was OK.
He'd protect me. Did anything else matter?

Sir, your bath is ready. Warm, but not hot. Would you permit me to assist you?

Yes, please, I answered. I doubt I could get into that tub or
get out without your help.

A long while later, after he had washed me very gently and
yet very thoroughly, Feng said, If you permit me to make this
observation, you have been horribly mistreated. I believe
you need medical care as well as a great deal of rest. Do you
remember Dr. Yan, sir?

After a moment of blankness, I said, Yes, I do. The doctor
who took care of my arm after my noncom Eric cut me, that
time when you saved my life.

Yes, the doctor who stitched up your arm. He would be
helpful. May I ask him to come?

Yes, I would like that.

Feng dried me, dressed me in flannel pajamas and a wool bathrobe, and asked, Will you have breakfast in the dining room or in bed?

In the kitchen, please.

He gave me scrambled eggs, which I could eat easily, and porridge.

This is so good, Feng, I said. I've been eating garbage. Real garbage. Rancid scrapings of the Monster's and his people's plates, I suppose. Or rotting garbage they collected elsewhere. I'd like some more.

I am so very sorry, sir, but you need to take small portions of nourishment until we accustom your stomach to eating real food and normal portions.

I understand. Could I take a look at the paper?

He put before me the first section of *The New York Times*.

I picked it up. Trump's face on the first page. That had not changed. Saying he will decertify the Iran agreement. Why not? Another brilliant move toward a general war in the Middle East. Perhaps beyond. I pushed the paper away.

Meanwhile, Feng was speaking over the telephone in Chinese. Dr. Yan will be here at one. You have time, sir, to rest before his visit.

The doctor had Feng undress me and examined me on my bed, front and back, poking and pinching. Every part of my body he touched hurt, the pain sometimes so sharp that I couldn't help crying out.

Each time he asked my pardon, with elaborate courtesy.

His diction was not unlike Feng's. Stiffer perhaps, although he had lived in the United States much longer. When he'd finished, he asked Feng to give me a cup of tea and said, With your permission, I will state my opinion.

Please do, I said, by all means.

You are quite unwell, sir. The wounds on your back have closed, but they are infected. I give you an injection of antibiotic and put antibiotic ointment on the wounds. I must apply light bandage that protects wounds and allow them to breathe. Feng or I will change the bandage as needed.

Thank you!

I recommend acupuncture to relieve pain and mental stress. I can perform acupuncture. With your permission, we will have first session today and will have session every day in the weeks to come until no longer needed. Will that be all right, sir?

Certainly, I'm most grateful.

You will need X-rays and MRI and perhaps CAT scan that your regular doctor will arrange. They are needed to discover whether there are injuries that my examination has not revealed. Your bones are not crushed. Orthopedic surgeon can reset your legs and feet correctly to enable you to walk with ease. Also, your fingers, if fingers are uncomfortable.

I'd almost forgotten my broken fingers. That had happened so long ago. Hands on the table and wham, a blow with a mallet. Was it the first day? That meant nothing. I couldn't tell day from night or when night changed into day. I'd hardly used my hands and looked at them now with something like curiosity. Gnarled. Would I be able to use those fingers to type? I wouldn't know until I tried. Would I have any reason to type?

I lay on my stomach for the acupuncture. Dr. Yan lit a candle on my night table that gave off a strong but pleasant smell.

It will help you relax, sir.

Perhaps it did. I fell into a deep and dreamless sleep. When I awoke, still on my stomach, I found that Feng or Dr. Yen had covered me with a light blanket. I felt pleasantly warm and comfortable. The analog clock on my Bosch radio and CD player showed 6:42. In the evening, I supposed. I needed to urinate, urgently. No, I hadn't wet the bed. I got up, saw that two Canadian canes had been placed against the armchair nearest my bed, and silently thanked Feng. That man really thought of everything and could get whatever was needed done. For instance, where in the Lord's name had he gotten those canes? Called one of the big drugstores, I supposed, and had them delivered, or perhaps Dr. Yan had told him I'd be asleep a good long while and he'd ducked out to buy them. He must have gone out with Satan as well.

He had put out a sweat suit for me. I did my business in the bathroom, rinsed my mouth, put on the sweat suit, and, feeling surer of myself as I leaned on the canes, I set out in search of Feng. He wasn't in the kitchen, and Satan's collar and leash were not in their usual place.

Aha! The essential evening walk. He would have left around six; they've surely gone to the park and will be back soon. On the kitchen table was a platter with smoked-salmon canapés. A sign, I said to myself hopefully, that Dr. Yan hasn't done anything foolish like telling Feng I couldn't drink. It was impossible to resist the canapés. I stole two of them, licked my fingers, and went into the library. Feng had turned the lights on, setting the dimmers exactly as I would have done myself. The CDs were in the disorder in which I had left them. The disc on top of the pile was *Das Lied von der Erde*. My memory for trivia wasn't gone. This was a great recording from the sixties: Klemperer, Christa Ludwig, and Fritz Wunderlich, the superb tenor who died much too young in a grotesque accident. Falling down the stairs at a friend's hunting lodge, for Christ's sake. Yup, some people have all the luck. I inserted the disc in the CD player. *Dunkel ist das Leben, ist der Tod,* he sang, *Das Firmament blaut ewig, und die Erde wird lange fest stehen . . . Du aber, Mensch, wie lang lebst denn du?* The firmament is forever blue, and the earth will long abide, but you, Man, how long will you live? Hah! In my case, much too long. That was the answer. Why hadn't I had a cyanide capsule in my mouth that I could crush between my teeth as soon as Heidi had been whisked off Louse Point Beach by her father's security? At ease, Captain Dana! How the hell would you have known she'd been whisked off given that they knocked you out the moment you'd seen her in the distance? As for why you didn't have the fucking capsule in your mouth? That question is on the level of Do bears shit in the woods? You didn't have it in your mouth because you didn't happen to possess such a capsule. They weren't part of a Marine Corps Infantry officer's kit! A Marine Corps Infantry officer was there to kill and—if it was his turn—to be killed. He wasn't there to do the towelhead's job for him. The better question, asshole, is why you didn't put yourself out of your misery later, say, after they'd flayed you, after they broke your legs but before they knocked out your teeth, as soon as you saw the fucking bed frame and the cute apparatus on wheels, like something in a dentist's office, and you understood it was *la gégène!* The setup for electrical-shock torture the French used on the FLN during the Algerian War. The one thing that my peace-loving philosophy-professor father who so liked the French could not forgive. *La gégène!* That philosopher warrior who had fought as a marine officer in Vietnam with sufficient bravery to earn the Silver Star and the Navy Cross held that the electric was the worst. No one, however brave, could resist it. Or overcome the fear. He was right. That's how the Monster made me kowtow. Yes, I knew I had a way out—one of many—while I still had my teeth. While I still had them, I could have bitten through my tongue and bled to death. Almost impossible to stop the hemorrhage, even if you catch it quickly. But I didn't. Why? I don't know. Most likely, it wasn't my karma. No, you idiot! You'd lost your teeth!

I lay down on the sofa and listened to the music. At some point I fell asleep.

Satan woke me up, licking my face. The Omega wristwatch that had been my grandfather's was taken from me. I didn't know the time, but I can't have slept very long. Christa was only at the beginning of the next song. *Mein Herz ist müde,* my heart is tired. . . . How apt! Had a benevolent hidden force guided me to the Mahler masterpiece? Satan decided to nestle with his head on my shoulder and a front paw thrown over my left arm so that I couldn't get away. That was what he had wanted and soon he was snoring, the sure sign of his satisfaction. This is like the old days, he thinks. Poor Frenchie! He doesn't know how much I have changed.

Feng had entered the library so quietly that I did not become aware of his presence until he spoke.

May I bring you a drink, sir? he asked. Also, canapés. Just the way you like them.

Thank you, Feng, I answered, I've already helped myself to a couple of your wonderful canapés and am eager to have some more. And yes, I'd like a bourbon. Not a martini. I'm not up to them. No ice and not too much bourbon. I had better ease into it. And please pour a drink for yourself and join me here in the library.

Thank you, sir.

He returned, helped me liberate my arm from Satan's embrace and sit up leaning against two cushions so that I could drink and eat without disturbing the dog, passed the canapés, of which I devoured three immediately, and handed me my drink. It was exactly what I had wanted and, I thought, needed, but I realized that even a little more of that stuff might put me under. A counterthought: Did it matter?

Feng talked about Satan, who had been in good health, the walks they had taken in the Ramble, around the Reservoir, and sometimes in the North Woods, the fun Satan had on Dog Hill when he took him there in the morning and let him off the leash. It was clear to me, though, there was something else he wanted to speak about but didn't dare to bring up. I thought I knew what was on his mind and decided to help him.

Shao-Feng, I said, by now you're my old friend. One of my

two best friends. Tell me frankly whatever it is that you want to tell me. Don't be concerned about offending me.

Thank you, sir. I would like to say that we were all very worried about you. Often, we thought we would never see you again. Miss Heidi, sir, cried every time she came here. She cried playing with Satan. And at table. With your permission, sir, I would like to call her and say that you have returned, that you are here. It will make her so happy. So relieved.

That was what I had expected.

Feng, I told him, you've seen what they've done to me, you've seen what I've become. I'm even worse off inside. I've only been back since this morning. I'm not ready to see Miss Heidi. I don't know when I will be ready. Yes, she should know that I'm back, and you may call her to tell her that, but please say that I'm not well, that I need rest—you will find the right words. The point is I can't see her now and I'm not sure I can talk to her now.

Yes, sir, I will do just that. And what about Mr. Scott Prentice and Mr. Joe Edwards and Mr. Moses Cohen?

You're right, we must tell them I'm back. Perhaps I can do it after you've called Miss Heidi.

Yes, business must be attended to, although I wondered whether I had the strength for those conversations. And Heidi? Would she not see pretty quickly that I was no longer the man she said she loved, with whom she wanted to have a child? Must we go through the Sturm und Drang of her making her way toward that inevitable conclusion? I was really too tired for it. As for me—did I love her? Any answer I might give to that stupid question would have to be equally stupid.

Yes, I felt better than this morning, but this much hadn't changed: my fear of being hurt and humble contentment at being allowed to be quiet in my nice, clean apartment, with Satan pressed against my side and Feng ready to protect me. That's all I really felt. I didn't believe there was anything more that I wanted or could bear to want.

I finished the last drops of my bourbon and decided to ask for another shot as soon as Feng returned. The counter-thought was right on target: it made no difference whether the booze put me under. Indeed, it was a consummation devoutly to be wished.

He came back, carrying the phone, and said, Miss Heidi would like to speak to you, sir.

He handed me the receiver. I resisted the temptation to say, Please hang up; that was not part of the deal. I took the unnerving object from his hand.

Hello, Heidi, I managed to croak. Yes, I'm back at Fifth Avenue. It's been a long time.

Jack, she replied sobbing, my darling Jack, I'm on my way, I'll be there in two, two and a half hours. I so want to be with you, Jack.

You don't know what you're saying. I'm horribly changed. Give it time, sweetie, give it time. You really mustn't come here tonight. I beg you! Please!

You can't stop me, she answered, suddenly giggling, which was a Heidi sound, so don't try. I know you're very tired. Have your dinner and take a little nap. I'll know how to wake you!

She hung up. What was I to do?

She's coming, I said to Feng. Please give me another drink

and make up the guest room so Miss Heidi can sleep there if she wishes.

Thank you, sir! Dinner can be ready as soon as you are ready. Egg-drop soup and steamed eggs, sir. Very tasty and very nourishing. You need to build up your strength, sir.

Feng enchanted me. This wasn't principally about "nourishing"; it was about what I could handle with my toothless gums.

Excellent, I replied. Please let me have another bourbon and give me back the telephone. I'll try to reach Scott and Joe. We'll call Moses tomorrow.

Scott did not answer his cell phone. Even though it was Saturday, most likely that meant he was in a meeting of some considerable importance. He checked his telephone compulsively, and I was sure that upon seeing my number he would have answered in all normal circumstances. Joe answered immediately.

It's really you? he asked.

Yes, it is.

And you're at your Fifth Avenue apartment?

Yes, since this morning.

Holy Jesus! This is what we were waiting for. Thank God! I've really got to go now, but I may have big news for you tomorrow.

I didn't lie down on my bed and close my eyes in obedience to Heidi's injunction. The fact is that I couldn't help it. After Feng's dinner and a glass of the Chinon he had opened—is it possible that I had forgotten how good food can taste?—I could not keep my eyes open. Fatigue, in my case, I was discovering, was a separate and excruciating wave of pain. Dr. Yan left a supply of a painkiller, Percocet, I think. I asked Feng for a tablet, stretched out, and, although that was hardly necessary, reminded him that Heidi was on her way.

She'll probably get here before midnight. I'm setting my alarm clock for eleven-thirty. Please wake me if she manages to get here earlier.

It's practical to have no teeth, I thought. No need to worry about brushing. A quick rinse with mouthwash, a splash of water on the face that's all scars—not from shaving—and a flattened nose, and this facsimile monster is good to go.

I don't know whether because Feng, who didn't want me to miss a minute of rest, turned off the alarm clock or, with my gnarled and stiff fingers I did not manage to set it, I was asleep, and it was just as Heidi had said. I was awakened by her, by her breath the sweetness of which even the brutalized animal I had become could not fail to recognize. She was on the bed, pressed against me, caressing my head. Jack, Jack, she kept repeating, I had hoped this day would come, and it has come, we are together. No, don't wake up, I'll stay here with you. We'll talk in the morning, the way we always did, over breakfast in bed.

No, darling Heidi, I said, really no, that's quite impossible. You don't know what I have become, you can have no idea. I can't allow you to find out when you open your eyes in the morning. It can't be.

Then show me now, she cried out, and turned on the bed-side lamp.

Oh my God!

Yes, and you've only seen some of it. My face. The eye they've plucked out. I'm toothless. My back and thighs have been flayed, and right now my back is covered with infected wounds from a whipping that have closed but are festering. My hands—look! They broke my shins and set them crooked. I can hardly walk without these—I pointed to the Canadian canes. They've also broken my feet. And there is nothing left inside me—only fear. I'm afraid of more pain, Heidi, I'm afraid of the Monster. Please, Heidi, please. Go away!

She sat up and said, Jack, please take off this sweat suit. I want to see for myself. And please turn on the overhead light.

I did as she said.

Your back, she whispered, under the bandages. It must be awful.

I believe it is.

This ghastly tattoo, your poor legs. Jack, you let them do all this for me.

No, I didn't. I was in a game I didn't want to be in, a game I didn't understand, I played badly, and I lost. You had noth-ing to do with it. He was after me, he wanted me alive, so he could do what he did. You and Jonjon were bystand-ers, pawns—momentarily useful to him. Even if that stupid brother of yours had never set foot in a casino, if Jonjon and his parents had stayed in Hong Kong, even if you hadn't gone with the kid to the beach, he would have taken me. Please,

Heidi, get this into your head: what happened to me did not happen because of you. It happened because I drove Abner Brown to kill himself. That's all. End of story. And I'll tell you an alternate ending to the story: I don't go to Louse Point. The Monster kills you and Jonjon, in your case in some awful way. What would be left for me to do except put a bullet in my head? He checkmated me in a game that isn't chess, a hellish board game of his invention. He is a prince of evil. Please, Heidi, get that into your head! Leave me! Forget me! You'll find someone else who is sound in body and in mind, a nice man or a nice woman, you will be happy in a normal way with a normal partner, and you will make me happy if you allow me to remain your friend.

Jack, she said after a moment, that's quite a speech. Thank you! I'm pretty sure Feng has gone to bed. Would it be all right if I sneaked into the pantry and got us each a nice shot of Oban?

I couldn't help smiling. Are you sure you can find your way? I asked.

You forget, Captain, I've been a regular presence here, keeping an eye on Satan and your nanny, Feng. Back in a jiffy!

I shut my eye and tried very hard not to think while she was away, to make my mind a complete blank, just as I had done during the flaying and under the *gégène*.

She tiptoed in, I didn't hear her, it was a kiss she deposited on my forehead that told me she had returned. I had not looked at her before, when she awakened me, and now saw that she must have gotten ready for bed before first coming in. She wore the silk pajamas she had on, and that I had so delighted in removing, the night she returned from Tokyo.

Here, my darling Jack, she said, here is the magic potion. Sit up to drink! I'll put some pillows under your back.

I did as she said. She sat cross-legged facing me, and smiled, smiled, and smiled.

Then she spoke.

There is a question I have for you. My rapid inspection did not reveal any injury to a certain essential part of you. Am I right about that?

If I understand the question, the answer is yes. The Monster considered castrating me and decided against it. Because he has not been castrated. To maintain the parity between us as he conceived it.

That is very good news, Captain, because of a declaration I'm about to make. Now hear this, Captain: I love you, I love every part of you, broken and unbroken, wounded and sound. I am going to marry you just as soon as we can get the license. You are going to give me a baby. And we're getting to work on that already tonight. So, drink up!

Epilogue

The big news that Joe Edwards had promised when I told him I was alive and at Fifth Avenue came the next morning while Heidi and I were having breakfast in bed. When I saw the call was from him, I put him on the loudspeaker. In fact, Scott Prentice was on the line as well. They were exultant to the point of speechlessness, and when they finally spoke they kept interrupting each other. The FBI, we learned, and the Agency had known where the Monster held me from the day after my capture, satellite photography having made possible the tracing of the motor yacht onto which I had been loaded from Louse Point to Pig Island, a postage-stamp-sized private island in Penobscot Bay.

This is highly classified U.S. operational capacity, Jack and Heidi, Scott interjected. Please don't speak about it to anyone. It's open season here on guys who leak.

There was one big house on the island, Joe continued, with some nondescript small structures near it. We had no doubt you were held on the island, sir, but the decision was made that if we attempted a landing, amphibious or by parachute or helicopter, they would immediately kill you. After hours of discussion—Scott was in on it—we decided to gamble. We gambled that once they were through doing whatever they were doing to you they'd let you go. We'd go in the moment that happened or anyway if they killed you. We gave ourselves six months. If you weren't out by then, we'd assume you were dead, and we'd let them have it. So as soon as I got your call, we gave operations the green light they'd been praying for, and at dawn they struck. By speedboat and helicopter. But as they approached, the place exploded. Literally exploded and burned. We'll be in there checking out the bodies or what's left of them as soon as the place cools down enough to make that possible.

A report a couple of weeks later on the debris found on the island was bitterly disappointing. There were bodies there, all right, but burned to the point that such DNA as could be harvested was not likely to be truly usable. Logically, there was no doubt the Monster was on the island. The surveillance satellite had detected no departures in the forty-eight hours that preceded my being taken off the island. So that was it: we had no hundred-percent assurance that the Monster was indeed Abner's twin or that his Cyclops eye would not be trained on me.

Except for a coincidence. Following my liberation, Interpol, the FBI, and the Hong Kong police came down hard on Yellow Flower, the triad that the Macao casino hired to collect its debt from Michael Krohn. As Joe Edwards put it, no Miranda warnings were issued when the casino manager who hired Yellow Flower or the triad members were interrogated. The trail to the subcontractor the triad had in turn retained to handle the American aspects of the problem, the operatives working for the Monster, led to Andorra la Vella, where surprisingly efficient Andorran cops confirmed the long-term residence in that tiny capital city of an immensely rich American by the name of Obadiah Brown, a personage so reclusive that the police chief had never seen him and was unable to find anyone who had, although numerous visitors went to the house, almost always after dark. His mountainside house was the largest in La Vella, perhaps in the country, and so closely guarded that curiosity seekers could not get closer to it than its barbed-wire perimeter fence. The extraordinary and puzzling fact the police chief reported was that at 1300 hours local time on the afternoon of October 15, 2017, the house literally exploded and burned in a conflagration so fierce that firefighters could not approach it. That happened to be the hour and date of the FBI's attempted raid on the Monster's Pig Island installation and its destruction in an explosion and a fire. The FBI's search of all possibly relevant records disclosed no trace of Obadiah Brown. The U.S. passport he had at one point exhibited to Andorra officials must have been a fake; property records showed that the house was owned by a Panamanian company organized in the early 1950s by a Panamanian lawyer who died some years later. The company's stock was represented by bearer shares that were impossible to trace.

It was possible then that I had been in a sense avenged;

what the Monster had done to me had led to his destruction
and the annihilation of his enterprise. It was also possible, I
thought, that he had not remained on Pig Island. Instead he
had accompanied the body bag in which I was transported
and saw it deposited at the foot of State Street. Then having
stepped into a waiting limousine, he traveled to the St. Regis
or the Pierre and checked into a presidential suite where he
has been watching X-rated films on TV and issuing orders to
his goons.

My kidnapping, I learned over the days that followed my
liberation, had been a media obsession and the subject of
at least two of the president's blasts. Weak corrupt FBI, he
tweeted. War hero kidnapped and FBI too busy with Collusion Witch Hunt to save him. Pathetic! My reappearance
ignited another media bonfire, but one of short duration
because my literary agent and Moses Cohen as my attorney
made it clear that I would not be available for interviews.
Moses issued the following statement on my behalf: Jack
Dana has been released from his captivity during which he
was exposed to extreme hardships. He is resting and receiving appropriate medical treatment. The FBI released a
statement to the effect that to the best of its knowledge the
kidnappers had all been killed in an explosion that occurred
in the course of a raid on the gang's hideout on Pig Island in
Maine.

Dr. Yan continued the acupuncture treatments for six
more weeks. In the meantime, arrangements were made for
undoing as much as possible of what the Monster had done to
me. My legs, feet, and hands were rebroken and reset; plastic

surgeons worked on my face, in my opinion with questionable success; I decided against being fitted with a glass eye. It was too much of a reminder of the words that passed between the Monster and me before he plucked my eye out. He had asked which of his eyes I liked more. The glass eye, I had replied. It looks human. That's good, fuckhead, he replied. You'll get to have one of your own. I was sure, I told the eye doctor, that an eyepatch suited me better.

For an outrageous price, an orthodontist implanted new and almost real-looking teeth on the stubs of my old ones.

A variety of tests, some of which I found comical, confirmed the absence of noticeable cognitive impairment.

The work on my wretched body and mouth was spread over many months. When it was finished, I resumed my work with Wolf, my martial arts trainer. We worked out daily and, to our mutual surprise, after a couple of months he pronounced me almost as good as I had ever been. I'd also gone to a shooting range to make sure that the loss of my left eye did not interfere with my marksmanship. It was the eye I normally closed when taking aim. I was still a good shot.

It seemed that it took no time at all for Heidi to restore my happiness and will to live. We followed her prescription.

Two weeks after my return to Fifth Avenue, we were married at the New York City Marriage Bureau. The wedding lunch at our apartment, for which Feng cooked up a storm, was attended by Scott Prentice; his wife, Susie, to whom I had introduced him; Joe Edwards and his wife; and Heidi's parents. Over Heidi's objections, I wore a black velvet Venetian mask. Don't want to spook our guests, I decreed. Our baby weighed 9.1 pounds at birth and was 22 inches long. The date of his arrival left little doubt as to the date of his conception: the magical night during which Heidi and I were reunited. We called the kid Scott, after his godfather and the brother I would have wished to have.

We didn't want Satan to feel relegated to the suburbs of our affection by little Scott's entry on the scene. Heidi found the solution: we brought home a black-and-white little Frenchie, three months old. For no particular reason, we named him Louis. Satan approved of the transaction. It was the friend he had always wanted.

After he learned that Heidi was pregnant but before little Scott was born, Jon Krohn had called on me several times. It was over my halfhearted objections that I attempted to transmit through Heidi. You have to let him visit you, she said finally. He has what he considers important matters to discuss with you. Don't forget that I see him almost every day now and have no place to hide when he starts nagging.

He had put her at the head of his companies, while he "stepped up," as he liked to say, into a nonexecutive chairmanship, a euphemism for retirement. Michael had been shipped back to Hong Kong to serve on the board of a foundation set up to preserve native music. The funding naturally was supplied by Krohn Enterprises, but Heidi told me that Chinese music was a subject he knew a good deal about, more than about fashion or manufacturing. He departed sans Lilly and sans Jonjon. The divorce decree gave Lilly and Jon Krohn joint custody of the kid (an unheard-of arrangement, according to Moses Cohen) and stipulated that unless Jon otherwise consented the kid would be brought up in New York City.

The matters Jon wanted to discuss with me turned out to be nothing less than reparations he thought he owed me. Would I prefer a handsome capital settlement or a seat on the executive committee of his top holding company, a position that would entitle me to emoluments in the higher range of seven figures? He owed me so much more.

For the first time in a long time I laughed so hard that a coughing fit followed. Jon, I said when I could speak, I have Heidi! I need nothing more! A pearl richer than all my tribe. She's the love of my life. Stop fretting. We split household expenses, and besides I can afford them even without her help.

But it was all my fault, he wailed. I didn't follow your advice.

No, I said, it wasn't your fault. It was a project the Monster had decided he would carry out. Nothing you might have done that Memorial Day weekend could have saved me.

Well, thank God at least the bastard is dead.

Most probably. Jon didn't know, and I didn't tell anyone, not even Heidi, Scott, Joe, or Feng, that shortly after little Scott was born, but before Heidi and the baby had come home from the hospital, I received an email on my polluted laptop Feng had brought from Sag Harbor and placed in my Fifth Avenue study. From habit that I think I will never break I consult it daily. The sender identified himself as the Teacher with an address that any idiot would recognize as the address of a phisher. I didn't care. That laptop was a latrine. Anyone, including the Teacher, was welcome to stop by and unload. I clicked on the email and read the following:

> The heart of the wise is in the house of mourning, but the heart of fools dwells in the house of mirth.

Ecclesiastes. I knew the text. Being educated at an Episcopal boarding school is not entirely useless. Abner could have sent that email, but as I had never tired of repeating, dead men who have been incinerated don't send emails. It was the Monster's form as well, but hadn't he burned to a crisp on Pig Island? I'd no doubt that the FBI would be unable to find the Teacher just as they had been unable to find the Monster before they pinpointed him on Pig Island. I wouldn't waste their or my time. Nor would I commit little Scott, Heidi, Feng, and our two little Frenchies to living in a bunker, not even a bunker as luxurious as the Krohn money could make it. That would be the true house of mourning, and it was not for us. We would live in the house of mirth however unfunny our world was becoming. Feng and I would keep watch, and with his help Heidi and I would raise the little boy to be strong and fearless.

I was turning this conclusion over in my mind when a new email appeared on the screen of my laptop. This one read as follows:

> You have received a text from the Holy Book as a service from the McClusky, ND, Society of the Faithful.

If you do not wish to receive further messages from us,
please click on the Unsubscribe link below.

Another flash of diabolical humor? I didn't think I cared.
With a grin on my still-toothless face, I followed the link and
unsubscribed.

A NOTE ON THE TYPE

This book was set in Hoefler Text, a family of fonts designed
in 1991 by Jonathan Hoefler, who was born in 1970. Hoefler
Text looks to the old-style fonts of the seventeenth century,
but it is wholly of its time, employing a precision and sophis-
tication only available to the late twentieth century.